22

My Enemy's Cherry Tree

My Enemy's Cherry Tree

Wang Ting-Kuo

Translated from the Chinese
by Howard Goldblatt and Sylvia Li-chun Lin

GRANTA

Published by Granta Books in 2019

Granta Publications
12 Addison Avenue
London
W11 4QR

A CIP catalogue record for this book is available from the British Library

9 8 7 6 5 4 3 2 1

ISBN 978 1 84627 658 3
eISBN 978 1 84627 660 6

Typeset by Avon DataSet, Bidford on Avon, Warwickshire

Printed and bound by CPI Group (UK) Ltd, Croydon, CR0 4YY

www.granta.com

I

We don't have to start if you're not ready

The late-morning coffee shop was empty. He was the first customer. He walked in wearing a tan bucket hat and stopped short, surprised to see that it was a one-man operation. I was all there was, no helper in sight.

It was too late to turn back. He took the seat nearest the door and, without removing his hat, sat staring woodenly out at the bicycle he had ridden over. The moment felt unreal. A gust of wind gently rattled the windowpane, creating a noise like an earth tremor.

The silence made it unnecessary for me to say anything or for him to place an order, so I reflexively brought out a cup and saucer. The small shop sank into an uncanny stillness the moment the mill began grinding beans.

He was on his feet before he'd finished his coffee.

Moving ahead of him, I opened the door and walked out. I didn't want to hear a word from him or take his money, so I went all the way to the junction to wait for him to leave. A long time passed and I assumed he was still inside. But when I looked back, I saw that he had walked out through the glass door and was sitting on a raised flowerbed under the overhang, drawing furiously on a cigarette that had burned down to the filter. His cheeks were sunken from the effort, but he refused to toss it away, like a gambler who has lost everything.

1

Luo Yiming went home after finishing that cigarette and, I heard, fell ill.

He went up to the roof of the house to sit in his wrought-iron chair, his favourite spot to read and gaze at the distant hills that clung to the bends in the river. It must have been early afternoon, though someone said that it was dusk. A neighbour was out gathering clothes drying on her balcony when she saw old Mr Luo abruptly stand and, as if following a cryptic order, climb onto the railing.

She screamed, drawing a stream of neighbours out of their houses. The neighbourhood warden called the local watch team, whose arrival blocked the squad car that drove up to the alley, so that the police could only watch from a distance. Mr Luo's face was ashen when he was finally helped down, his legs still quaking, but he refused to answer any questions. All anyone heard was the woman crying as she repeated to the police what she had witnessed: she'd seen a flock of pigeons soar into the air, the most she'd seen since moving in five years before.

Several days later, when I was at the market, I was given a noticeably cooler reception by shop owners I knew fairly well. Street vendors resting on their haunches did business with me, but few were friendly enough to look up. It wasn't until I had moved on after making my purchases that they turned to talk to one another. I left quickly, head down, like a guilty man, for the town seemed to be quietly but unanimously expressing its anger at me.

There were a few occasions when people came up to talk. I didn't know them, but they obviously shared a common emotional bond, for they started each conversation by expressing their concern for Mr Luo Yiming, praising him as the town's philanthropist, a man who was approachable and compassionate in his dealings. The homeless often gathered outside his house, for Luo *San* would always come out and give them something to eat.

This talk of Luo Yiming's charitable acts wasn't idle gossip. According to a friend who volunteered at an NGO, at the end of each month Luo withdrew money from the credit co-op and stuffed it into envelopes. Putting aside those he sent to public charities, which had to be sent by registered mail, he placed the rest of the envelopes, big and small, in his cycle basket and delivered them by hand, like an industrious Santa Claus, creating a festive mood in the coastal town not unlike that of the New Year celebrations.

I was also told the heart-warming story of the new postman who had tried to deliver a letter to the Luo residence while he was off attending a wedding banquet. Neighbours heard the postman shouting three times outside the house that he had a letter for an 'anonymous recipient', and by the name on the envelope, they knew that it was a donation receipt.

Despite Luo *San*'s desire for anonymity, his good deed was found out, and, through the new postman's lack of discretion, his moving reputation as a secret benefactor had been confirmed.

After Luo fell ill, everything he had meant to the people was reheated like leftover food. All their praise flowed together to form a tune that played on the streets day and night, retaining its endearing warmth even with repetition, although now, when I think back to it, I feel only a contrasting sense of sadness.

But without a doubt, when I first met Luo Yiming, I too was filled with respect for the man. I was even convinced that without him in our society, our humanity would be incomplete; that without his graceful demeanour we would be denied a model of benevolence.

Even when what happened later totally destroyed the life I'd just begun, I didn't breathe a word of it to anyone. Society needs harmony. While the town continued to bathe in the illustrious glow of its hero, I shared everyone's hope that he would make a full recovery. For only when he was clear-headed enough to feel, now and then, the irony contained in the people's applause and experience the torment of someone else's pain would he recall the one man who could never forgive him.

And the truth is, my heart was tied in knots, and pain bored into the marrow of my bones when I heard about his illness. Honestly, I was heartbroken.

2

The Luo house I visited was a rare old building in the town, in that it had not got a single ceramic tile. It was built with metal features, aged wood, and stone from Yilan, and topped with black roof slates. Propped up by a great many stilts, the two-storey structure floated three metres above its foundations; an extensive veranda with creaky wood flooring ran across the front of the house above the garden.

I recall what Luo Yiming said when we first met, seven years ago: *This is a property passed down through the generations, I'm only its caretaker, not its owner. I have to wait till I retire to have the good fortune of making it my home.*

Though he played it down, I admired his background and experience. He was an important figure in a major commercial bank which itself had a decisive role in the financial sector. He was in charge of loans throughout central Taiwan. To put it mildly, he was someone who enjoyed both high status and great power. During the week, he resided in a flat owned by the bank, only returning to the family home on weekends and holidays.

For him, coming back here was a holiday, though he spent only a night in the house each week and usually had only a brief morning to work in the garden. When Qiuzi and I arrived that first time, he had already raked the fallen leaves into a pile and swept the ground. He quickly washed his hands in the pond so that he could escort us into the house through the veranda.

He wiped his forehead as he chatted with us. His striped shirt was soaked in sweat and his feet were still clad in short yellow rubber boots. We followed him inside, where he disappeared briefly and re-emerged in a white shirt and clean black trousers. His shirt was buttoned up to his throat, making the slack flesh of his neck quiver when he talked.

To me he seemed noble and yet unpretentious, an upright person at first glance. I was spellbound by the aura of the house, and particularly grateful for his enthusiasm, for I had to wonder who ordinarily could expect to enter a place like this – certainly not us. After only two visits I was already entertaining a base thought: I wished he were my father. The only possible explanation for this absurd notion was my actual father's inability to help me when my childhood illusion was shattered.

Qiuzi seemed more eager to visit the Luo residence than I was. She'd enrolled in a free photography tutorial he was giving, and that was how we had found ourselves with the privileged status of guests at this ancient abode of the super rich. Not everything about my wife was likeable, but she was uniquely persistent in the things she was learning, including her new hobby. She was childishly giddy in front of this expert, her eyes shining bright in Luo's class, oblivious to the possibility that a camera lens can sometimes be imperfect and miss the tough questions in life. Most likely, her purity had impressed

Luo Yiming and caused him to treat her like a daughter. I didn't think that anyone could casually enter the house of such a wealthy man.

She was happy to learn from Luo, of course, but I too tried hard to enjoy the visits, for I was concerned about my lack of sophistication. Whenever Manager Luo extended one of his generous invitations, no matter how difficult it was for me to get away, I managed to leave the construction site in Taipei County and rush back to Taichung, where I sped on towards his house in Haikou, with my wife on the back of my motor scooter. We would shout happily into the wind, loud enough to drown out the engine. With her arms around my waist, we bravely forged ahead, the wind in our faces, buoyed by the love of newlyweds.

Qiuzi normally sat by the telephone in Luo's living room, while he sat in a chair to her right. Gesturing constantly at the photos in his album, they talked animatedly, like two fish sizzling in a pan. Luo enjoyed sharing tales from his early years studying photography and showing some of his favourite photos, transforming the table into a mini photo exhibition. The newspaper and ashtray were swept out of the way, in the same way that I was relegated to the sidelines, happy to be ignored.

Generous with his advice, Luo explained photographic concepts and techniques to Qiuzi as he stood by the window like a thoughtful elder. Holding a series of negatives up to the light, he spoke as if to a captivated audience, absorbed in the details of his own coaching. With his salt and pepper hair, he had a beguiling presence.

As for me, my ignorance at the time meant I could only browse the photographs, for it is an art form that requires passion if it is to be discussed intelligently. Luo's house was huge, more spacious than any dreamworld. The architecture was Japanese in style and gave the building the air of an official residence. The subtle fragrance of aged wood was ever present, and I wondered how that sort of ambience would affect most people. They might feel a sense of despair, be filled with shame at their own inadequacy. But not me. A glint of jealousy existed, sure, but that was soothed by my imagination; I wasn't yet forty, and if Luo stopped to wait for me, I would have at least two decades in which to catch up with him.

As my imagination ran wild, I sat waiting for Qiuzi, an eager learner. Sometimes she asked odd questions. Take the darkroom, for instance. She wondered aloud if she needed to enter it wearing dark clothes. Or black-and-white photos. 'What do I do when, um, the camera lens captures a colourful bird?' Her desire to learn exposed many weaknesses, which were manifestations of her innocence, such as the purity of her neck exposed beneath her short hair. When a faint frown appeared on her face, which was like a clean sheet of paper, she looked as if she had been carelessly soiled by dust from the adult world.

But I liked Qiuzi the way she was. It was better to be slightly stupid than to be smart, for that allowed for the possibility of learning from others, unlike a clever mind that stagnates in its egotistical calculations. Actually, she wasn't stupid; she just displayed a hint of foolishness, a trait that made me love her all the more. I myself had lost all traces of purity and innocence. She lit up my shadow, relieving a certain heaviness in my life.

Which is to say, I couldn't live without Qiuzi. I was happy only when I saw her smile, and I shared in the praise and favour given to her. Holding a cup of hot summer tea in both hands, she listened quietly to her teacher, eyes blinking constantly on a face that radiated joy. She often laid down the cup to pick up her notebook and say, *Please slow down, Laoshi, so I can take better notes.*

I was sure she also provoked strong feelings in Luo Yiming. A man with a natural grace, he was reserved in many ways. When he was pleased, he smiled faintly, his teeth hidden, happiness stealing into his raspy voice. On our first visit, he enthusiastically invited us to stay for lunch. Knowing that he lived alone, however, we declined the invitation after exchanging glances. If everything had ended on that day, it would have been one of our most unforgettable moments. Unfortunately, however, we returned for a second visit not long before the flower season. The big cherry tree beyond Luo's window, still canopied in green leaves, had yet to bloom, its dark purple branches glowing enigmatically in the lightly shaded garden.

When she left me, the cherry tree was in bloom, and we lost that spring together.

3

Luo Yiming's sudden illness created quite a commotion.

Two policemen from the local station arrived, one speaking in the local Haikou accent, while the other, likely a rookie, began to rifle through the shop the minute he walked in. He gave out an odd cry when he spotted the curtain hanging from the low ceiling, as if he'd stumbled upon a drug den; he was so tense I thought he might draw his weapon.

After telling me to bring him a ladder, he nimbly climbed up it to reach the dark, cramped loft, where he paused, obviously unsure whether or not he should proceed. Probably itching to show off his athletic skill, he surprised me by pulling himself up into the opening, using the boards around the sides like parallel bars. His head preceded his audacious body and banged against the dark ceiling, producing a loud thud.

The ladder tilted to one side, leaving his upper body still in the loft, legs dangling. Haikou Accent steadied the ladder to help him down. His cry of pain having tempered to a moan, he rubbed his head and looked daggers at me. The scene had become almost farcical. I poured two glasses of water, placed them on a table and waited for the interrogation to begin.

'What's going on?' Rookie asked, miffed, still rubbing his head. 'What's up there?'

'A bed, a pillow and a radio.'

'Everyone in town says you came for revenge, and that's how I see it too.'

Haikou Accent concurred. 'People are saying your coffee shop is just a front. I tend to agree. Selling coffee here makes no sense. Why don't you offer herbal tea on a hot day like this?' He spoke consolingly to the injured head next to him as he entered the details from my ID card into his device. While we waited for its feedback, he copied my data onto a notepad.

He leaned close to me, the device having sent back its information.

'All right, you don't have a record. But what is it with you? What are you doing here, anyway?'

'I'm just here to sell coffee.'

'There are plenty of empty storefronts in town.'

'I'm close to the ocean here.'

'Like hell you are! Have you seen any crabs around this dump?' he snorted. 'Don't even think about lying to me. Anything relating to Mr Luo is our business. Have you got a grudge against him? Let me put it this way: are you really here for revenge? Because to be honest with you, I can't wait for some real action to save me from a shit career catching petty thieves. So go ahead and do what you want, turn the town inside out, just so long as you leave him alone. Our Mr Luo, he's the only person in this town who cannot die, and you'd better make sure he lives, so that I can breathe easy.'

Two customers entered and paused at the door. Haikou

Accent put his cap back on and, walking ahead of Rookie, turned to whisper:

'If anything happens to him I'll be back.'

After making and serving the drinks, I slipped outside and sat on a bench to smoke, feeling somewhat deflated. It was just a little shop I had there, dispensing a cup of coffee every now and then, but it would stay right where it was even if coffee one day disappeared from the face of the earth. I'd keep it open for my Qiuzi.

Truly, I had not expected Luo Yiming to barge in. From a distance I saw a bicycle passing slowly by; the rider looked ordinary, like some old villager. How could I have known that he would get off his bike and send me into sorrow, fear and despair? I couldn't tell if his arrival was the portent of a new disaster or a mere spectre.

He looked healthy, and I wondered why he had taken early retirement. He was obviously still robust enough to ride his bike all the way here. To him it was a carefree outing, much like an idle stroll, during which he would pause at spots he'd previously overlooked and take in interesting, unique, or dreamlike scenes of beauty. He was enjoying every day of his post-retirement life more than anyone else could.

Besides, having a cup of coffee was commonplace to him. His favourite coffee had a musky aroma, no sugar added, the black liquid enlivened by a profound imagination. Back then we'd sat in his living room, trying to savour its bitterness. The complexity of the coffee was lost on Qiuzi, and I too failed to grasp its far-flung flavours, of course. Too timid to make a sound, I fearfully held the golden saucer tight and tucked my arms in close, afraid that the expensive elegance of the coffee would expose my undue anxiety. We did know, however, that we were expected to quickly sniff out its worth. Instead of praising it in familiar, comfortable tones, we were to approach the coffee with a sense of bitter sorrow towards life, in order to wholeheartedly welcome its complexity into our hearts, from where the image of a lonely soul would arise. Then we were to suppress a furtive belch and let it linger shyly between our underactive oesophagus and our throat.

And so, on this ill-fated morning, he came only for a cup of coffee. He'd surely heard about a fool from out of town opening a little coffee shop in the remote outskirts of this desolate place. On this day, with nothing special in mind, he had taken one of his usual carefree cycle rides, and, since it was not yet lunchtime, had decided to stop for a cup. That must have been how it was.

If he hadn't made such a spur-of-the-moment decision, everything would have been the same as before, and he and I wouldn't have been simultaneously hurled into sorrow, fear and despair. He could have quietly stayed in the dark, where there was little trouble, since darkness is harmless. Only during a confrontation do we experience the sudden fear of losing ourselves when we cannot see our adversary, at which time darkness is tinted with terror and threatens to push both sides into a bottomless abyss.

Unlucky, then, that he set out. He may have ridden along the embankment on a little path that curved abruptly before leading to a bridge. To reach the Luo residence, which was located on the far side of the bridge, you passed by the Catholic church in the centre of town. It was close to the amusement park, and from its grassy slope you could see his ancient Japanese-style house, with its old cherry tree in full bloom.

As he slowly rode over on the shaded path, ah, what was

I doing at the time? Maybe I was getting ready to open or wiping down the empty bar. In any case, there was no sign from heaven, nor did my eyelids twitch to alert me, so naturally I had no inkling that we would soon meet under very awkward circumstances.

As he reached the spot below the embankment where the path curved upward, he would have whistled out of tune, as was his habit. If he'd had a sudden ominous premonition, he would still have had time to turn back. There were plenty of places he could have roamed. He could have ridden into an alley that would have taken him back to the town's old streets, or he could have pedalled through the bustling fruit and vegetable market, following the lumber mill's access road.

Regrettably, he did neither. Just as, when the opportunity arose to live out his life with honour, he let it pass.

4

A strange event occurred hard on the heels of the police visit. During an afternoon thunderstorm, a taxi pulled in and stopped on the gravel drive. The driver, umbrella in hand, ran round to open the back door, but it burst open before he got there, an impatient long skirt stepping out and bolting into the downpour, ignoring the proffered cover.

It was a woman who looked to be in her thirties, and she ran with fierce determination towards the overhang. But her heels caught in the gravel and sank back in as soon as she pulled them up. She kicked them off when she reached the door, where she sat down on the bench, crossed her legs, and repeatedly thumped the mud off the soles.

I was surprised, not just that she was a stranger, but also by her obvious disguise. Her face was heavily powdered and rouged, her hair held by a shiny purple band. A pair of bizarre dark glasses had slid down and hung precariously on her nose.

She could have been a tourist, but then someone with such heavy make-up would normally come in a sightseeing bus or be travelling with friends, not as a woman on her own.

It would make no sense to think that she was local. There was a pitifully small number of coffee drinkers in town, and none who would have braved the storm in such a way, especially with this affectation of such a peculiar appearance. Local residents dressed much more conservatively.

I was still at the counter, slightly bewildered, when she walked in and sat down by the window. The sunglasses had returned to their proper place, but could barely hide her indignation. When I greeted her with a glass of water, she sneered icily:

'Only an outsider would open a shop at a spot like this.'

I reacted to her scorn by surveying my surroundings. She was right. It was a terrible site for a coffee shop, not far from a dilapidated brick kiln and an embankment on the far side of the path. A nearby ditch filled with silt that had washed up from the Zhuoshui River waited for a flood to take it to the sea. The arrival of night would sweep away everything save the silent undercurrents that reverberated in my head, but they didn't come from the ocean, for it was two kilometres away.

So I could only respond with an awkward smile, unoffended by what she said. Frankly, she looked a mess, with drops of rainwater sliding down her hair, which framed a face smudged with make-up and looking haggard.

'Do you live here alone?' she asked.

I pointed to the ceiling above the bar, at which she made a disbelieving noise and smiled coolly, clearly doubting that anyone could live up there. Maybe she was right. It made no sense to build a loft beneath a standard-height ceiling, creating an enclosed space only four feet high, but that's what I'd done. Whenever I reached over to take something out of a cupboard, if I wasn't careful I scraped the bottom of the loft, almost as if I were touching my own back in the space where I slept each night.

Not surprisingly, a look of contempt appeared on her face as she stood up, walked over to a corner, and then turned back, as if she'd seen a hornets' nest and was getting ready to flee in case they decided to attack.

'Do you fly up there when you go to bed?'

'I use a ladder, of course. I put it away in the morning when I open for business.'

Not satisfied with my answer, she turned to glance at the abandoned kiln nearby. The rain had stopped, but she refused to leave. After she had examined the crowded space further, her temper flared, turning her smudged face bright red. Her pointed chin was quivering uncontrollably.

'Why, just why did you have to come to *our* place?'

Ah, that is the question.

When the irate woman left, I followed my routine of wiping down the tables and mopping the floor, before carrying the ladder over to climb into the loft. The space was the size of two tatami mats, big enough for me to lie down. More problematic was the need to lower my head as I crawled in; I had to remember to tuck my neck in or I'd bang my forehead against a ceiling that was barely high enough for a child to sit in and put on his trousers. For a fully grown man in his forties to do so, he would have to mimic the squiggles and squirms of a worm. Even a puppy would find it difficult to move around in a crevice that was as confining as its own fate.

Something different crept into my routine that night. When I was on my way up, I had a nagging feeling that I was missing something. I even stopped midway for a further exam-ination of my tiny space. Everything was in its rightful place, so I scrolled though my memory, and recalled that afternoon's brief thunderstorm, the angry long skirt, as well as the smug voice coming mostly out of her aristocratic nose.

Which is to say, the recollection evolved slowly only after I was up in my loft.

I was already in bed, but I couldn't wait, not even for a minute, so I had to worm my way back out of the inky black space. Face down, I slowly, carefully placed my feet on the top rung of the ladder and, by wriggling my rear end, pushed myself out, using my hands as leverage. My slow movements that night were so uncoordinated I nearly knocked the ladder down.

What I couldn't wait to confirm was contained in my journal entry for the day we first met Luo Yiming. Only partially filled, my journal luckily had drifted with me and ended up locked away in a drawer downstairs. If my memory was correct, that woman could be found in its pages. Even a rough sketch would be enough to peg her as a member of the Luo family. Time had passed, but a journal doesn't lie, unlike a disguise that had taken me hours to see through.

Wasn't she the girl who had hidden upstairs, home from Taipei on a break?

Opening the drawer, I took out the journal and flipped to July of that year, 23 July.

To my disappointment, the entry started with: *Visited the Luo residence, a stifling hot, windless day.*

For some reason, I seem to have been in a funk that day, because the handwriting was sloppy. I had just brought Qiuzi home from our visit to the Luo house, hadn't I? Ah, did I already have a dark side that, despite the smile on my face, showed itself that night in a journal entry where words failed me? Otherwise, I would surely have described my feelings, since everything I'd seen that day at the Luo home – from the veranda by the door to the cherry blossoms in the garden and the elegant interior décor – was perfect material for a journal entry. More importantly, the woman who showed up today must have been the girl on the stairs. The open staircase was clear in my mind's eye; she had obviously been spying on us through a space between the steps. When she realized I had spotted her, she sprang up, her bare feet tiptoeing on the stairs and disappearing with catlike silence.

Our days pass all too quickly, but certain dates remain once their footsteps are imprinted with words, arousing unusual responses at certain moments in time. Like now. She had grown into a mature woman, but her slender figure was frozen in my memory of that day, as if meeting her just that one time had focused the impression sharply.

For some strange reason, in the blank space below those terse lines, I'd drawn a circle containing the character for water. Why water? Had I felt something flow away that night? The ink itself had run at the time, as if the tiny character overflowed with wordless sorrow.

What a terrible association – it finally came to me. She had vaulted up the stairs, a glass of water in her hand. The transparent glass reflected dim light from the window, while its contents rippled slightly in her attempt to get away, even sprinkling her calves as she made a quick retreat.

I hadn't expected those calves to walk up to me on this day.

They must have stomped angrily along the way; she kept banging her muddy shoes together after stopping under the eaves.

5

To my surprise, the woman who walked out of the journal showed up again the very next morning.

She came in slowly after first rapping on the glass door, her expression relaxed, her anger seemingly washed away by the rainstorm of the day before. If I may be frank, she struck me now as a pretty woman, her dark eyes shining brightly on an unadorned face with a fair complexion. I could almost see the graceful figure that had descended the stairs years ago, so far removed from our encounter the day before, when I had only been able to see her chin in all its pointed fury.

She handed me a business card with her name, Luo Baixiu, printed on it, proving beyond doubt that I had guessed right. I had to feel sorry for her. Worried sick by her father's illness, she must have taken time off to come home, only to see his situation worsen. And so, after a night of torment, she had no choice but to modify her foolish behaviour and return in a less confrontational manner.

As a form of apology, she spoke softly and kept her head

low, her hair gathered behind her neck with a butterfly clip. Assuming that I knew everything, she sat down and came straight to the point.

'We took my father to the hospital again last night. They had to restrain him before the doctor could examine him. After we got home, he took his medicine and finally went to sleep, but woke up before long, threw on some clothes, and was ready to run off to who knows where. He was wide awake throughout the rest of the night.'

As she related the episode, she fixed her gaze not on my eyes, but on my fingers, as if it was that hand that had pushed her father into a desperate situation. Those fingers, more articulate than my mouth, were able to speak for me, tapping the table gently as though sounding out a familiar tune. In fact, I made the meaningless noise simply because I was caught in a dilemma.

'Did my father really come here just for a cup of coffee?'

'Likely he was passing through and just walked in on the spur of the moment.'

'What did you say to him?'

'Nothing. I didn't say a word.'

'That's it, then. Why didn't you? Your silence must have frightened him.'

Miss Baixiu pursed her lips, as if she had found a clue from my tapping fingers.

'I'm sure you've heard how he conducts himself. He's an upright man, someone who cannot allow himself to make even a tiny mistake.' This she said to a shadow on the window. 'For a while before I went to college, I washed his shirt every day, and saw that it wasn't creased at all. It must have been hard on him, sitting rigidly at his desk day in, day out; he's lived a cautious life. I'm his daughter, but I don't know how to help him when something like this happens.'

'He *is* an upright man.'

'And,' she continued proudly, holding back her tears, 'my mother died giving birth to me. Over the decades that followed, anyone else would have remarried, but not him. He quietly made it through, year after year, all alone, and I never heard a word of complaint from him. What I dreaded most when I came home over breaks was how he insisted on seeing me off at the train station. Can you imagine him standing on the platform like a soldier, his hand in the air, a sorry, lonely figure? People probably thought his daughter was leaving home for good.'

I mumbled a reply without interrupting her. I really didn't feel like listening, so I turned to look out the window at the shadows of passing birds, and then gazed into the distant sky, where dark clouds were brewing up another rainstorm. As I did so, I felt her observing my face; she blinked and lowered her head when I turned back to her. She fixed her uneasy gaze on my fingers once more.

In her eyes, I must have seemed guilty, which was why she was so jumpy, so touchy. Let her finish in peace then, I said to myself. Her narrative will surely eclipse the noisy rumours swirling in the neighbourhood. Luo Yiming should be pleased. Where had he found the time to get sick, when his daughter was covering him with a coat of kindness and emphasizing his upright, loving and lonely image, as if it had been vividly silhouetted against a spotless paper window?

I took advantage of her steady gaze on my hand to study her profile. Her lips were on the thin side and partly pursed at the corners, as if weighed down by worry, adding charm to the shaded curves of her mouth. What a pity that a woman who looked like her had not changed out of her long skirt. A simple skirt would have worked better, emphasizing her lovely figure, as she slightly bared her shapely knees, in much the same way as her father would have come across as more straightforward and sincere if he'd left the collar button of his shirt undone.

'A man from the temple called to say that he'd made a large donation and then had just stood there holding the receipt instead of waving goodbye as he usually would have done. Turns out he wanted to sign the donation book. He'd never publicized his good deeds in the past. What's happened to him? The man also said it took my father a long time to write the top part of our name, and then his hand began to shake. That scared me. As you know, our surname has two parts. When he finally added the bottom half, it came out as Zui, the character for sin. He wrote it too big for the signature box, it filled the space.

'Say something,' she continued, 'otherwise it's like you're getting back at him. Why didn't you talk to him that day? He'd have been all right if you had. You did it on purpose. What did you have in mind anyway? You opened a coffee shop here just to scare him, didn't you? The nights are long, and it's so dark around here. What do you do? You really like the ocean that much? You can't even hear it from here. There are plenty of other places with better views. I passed through here once, when I was little. Our car roared down the road with no plans to stop.'

Qiuzi was her age when she left me, her face had had the same youthful glow. She had used simple words and had often sounded like a chirping sparrow, with a soothing, sunny effect, giving the impression of dull innocence. In comparison, Miss Baixiu seemed to have been through a lot and was under a heavier emotional strain. Even if she wanted a normal conversation, anxiety would creep into her voice before long, in much the same way that the sorrowful look on her lips turned her smile sad and her complaints aggressive.

'I talked to a doctor in the county hospital's psychiatric ward who told me it was a form of self-torment. But why, and for how long must he suffer? Has he committed a crime? If so, or if you believe he has, then tell me.'

'Miss Baixiu, I really had no idea he would be like this.'

'Who did? Yesterday he got up in the middle of the night for something to eat, but halfway through he put down his chopsticks. I thought he'd finally decided to tell me what was going on, but no. He pointed to his throat, unable to speak. Turns out there was a fish bone stuck in there. I grabbed a flashlight and shone it down his open mouth to help, but tears were streaming down his face before I could find the bone.'

'Did you find it?' I couldn't help myself.

'The bone isn't that important, is it? I've already told you more than enough.'

Miss Baixiu finally let tears brim over and roll down her cheeks. She gripped a white handkerchief tighter and tighter. Her sad little fist trembled helplessly, but she wouldn't let go.

It appeared to me that she had come to confess, what with her talk of atonement, torment and a fish bone. If she kept going, I wouldn't have been surprised if there had been more tears. So I got up and walked over to the bar, where I rewashed a rag that had already been cleaned and dried, unplugged the coffee mill and strolled outside listlessly before coming back.

Then I took the coins out of the cash register, counted them, and put them back one at a time. Her eyes were fixed on my back the whole time I was performing these meaningless tasks; I could sense the anticipation in her gaze, which had me thinking that a lack of options in life wasn't necessarily tragic. It is always nice when someone comes to confess, but she had to do so with sincerity, with the honesty of true love. Miss Baixiu would have to reveal everything she'd learned from her spying that year. I wanted nothing less than a full disclosure of her father's secrets.

Naturally, in the end she held back. Someone happened to walk by as she was leaving. He looked like a friend of her father's, and they started talking by the roadside. Soon she was crying again, her hand covering her nose and mouth, while the man appeared to be consoling her. He abruptly turned to glare at the coffee shop sign.

I didn't go out much those days. When I needed supplies, I did my best to restock at the market before sunrise. I heard less gossip that way, but the declining business at the coffee shop was impossible to turn around. With Miss Luo Baixiu's tearful loss of control out on the road, I expected all my customers, however few there were, to sooner or later flow away like her tears.

Clearly, I couldn't live by the shop alone. Sometimes I only sold two drinks from morning to closing time, and a typhoon would mean shuttering it for at least three days. There was, of course, something special about my body. If I suddenly stopped breathing one day, a doctor would never find the cause of my death; he would, instead, be astonished to find my organs alive and well, in addition to all the stubborn blood cells continuing to race determinedly through my veins. They were so bothered by Qiuzi's absence that, like me, they would refuse to depart.

That was how I made it through each day. Monks renowned for their spiritual enlightenment still need a drink of water, while I believed that waiting for her alone would keep me going.

6

That is to say, years ago, when she was still an innocent young girl, Miss Luo Baixiu had caught sight of her father's mysterious back, which was why she had rushed over to ask for my help when he fell ill.

Sadly, Qiuzi and I had been ignorant of what our future held. Each time we left the Luo residence, we strolled through the town's ancient streets and enjoyed the local shrimp balls and oyster pancakes. Usually, we were having so much fun we weren't ready to go home straight away, especially Qiuzi, who didn't get out much.

'Let's go to the beach,' she said one day, patting the camera in her backpack in high spirits.

'Be prepared to be disappointed,' I said, 'I hear the beaches around here are covered with silt. There's no sand. And they're inaccessible, since the embankment was declared a restricted area when it was under military control.'

'That's outrageous. The waves must find it hard to breathe.'

'What do you mean? They could stop, and everything would be fine.'

'Idiot. The waves would have trouble finding the beach. You said that yourself.'

As I turned in the direction of the ocean, a strong fishy odour emanated from the trees in the stuffy, hot windbreak. But not even the bumpy dirt road could dampen our spirits. I would never let Qiuzi go anywhere alone, not to heaven and not to hell. Besides, going to the Luo residence gave her a rare chance to get out of the house, where she spent most of her time. She would usually be dozing on the sofa when I came home on the night train each week.

It was just a trip to the beach, but I knew, of course, that ever since taking Luo Yiming's tutorial, she was always in search of a few good photos for her teacher's approval. We were still bouncing down the road when she removed the camera from its leather case and held it tightly to her chest, gently stroking it like a pet and talking to it: *Be good, don't be scared. I hear there's no sand on the beach.*

I tried to slow down so she could carefully remove the lens cover and focus her camera on the peanut field beside the road. When I turned to look at her, the setting sun was shining down on her lightly freckled face. A dainty dimple danced on her cheek. Looking as if she had been sucking on a preserved plum, she gave me a provocative, mischievous smile.

A petite woman, Qiuzi was not especially short, but she had a slight frame. The skin and muscles down her back created the world's most beautiful curves. If forced to find any fault, I would choose the moment when she would undress and reveal, albeit briefly, a tiny childhood scar hidden on the side of her left breast. Even after our love had turned us into husband and wife, she was always acutely conscious of the scar when we were in bed. She would bashfully keep the area hidden by lying on her side to cover it with her arm or by pressing it under her armpit. It was off limits to my hands, even to my furtive glances.

Qiuzi made love with only her right breast. As her husband, I naturally felt terrible about what she must have gone through to be scarred like that. Whenever we were not together, my first thoughts were not of her figure, but of the small breast tucked away under an elbow, calling out to me like a sad eye.

So had she tried a similar tactic when she was with Luo Yiming? Maybe. Since he was someone soon to be forgotten, she could let herself go for the moment, exposing her confined, embarrassing secret and lying down more freely on a bed that I couldn't see.

What would Luo Yiming have said? How did you get that scar? Does it still hurt?

The loss of the person we love the most takes with it our entire being. As the years passed, my memory of the secretive spot on her body slowly faded, and yet I was overwhelmed by irrepressible sorrow whenever I saw someone hold up a camera to take a picture. I hated both the way the cheek tilted to one side and the expression of concentration on the object. I was not so much doubtful of the breast's loyalty as I was fearful of the camera, that gloomy instrument. It would be aimed at someone I didn't know, a total stranger, but it always gave me the feeling that its dark lens was staring at my sorrow.

In particular, a clunky SLR camera inevitably, and for no reason, put me in a daze; I sensed that she was blinking behind every one of them that I came across, with Luo Yiming standing beside her, helping her adjust the lens and pointing out something in a colourful world that had suddenly turned chaotic. He leaned closer and closer as he kept making adjustments – the way she was standing, her fingers, her faint breathing, and her hair blowing in the wind.

For sure, nothing had yet happened when we first went to Luo Yiming's house or afterwards, when we rode down to the beach. If the road had branched off, it would have been only a fork in the road; no one could have known that it would soon lead to a dark grove of trees, especially not when the delightful scenery along the way charmed us and filled us with joy.

We came to the spot where the coffee shop would be.

An embankment had been built along the stream by then, and the spot was deserted, as if long forgotten by the town. Nothing grew on the embankment but reeds whose flowers swayed in the wind. She tapped my shoulder, getting me to stop.

'Look. The reeds are waving, like lovers who are about to part.'

She clicked the shutter, a young girl's dolefulness on her face, as she jested, 'If you leave me, I'll come here to wait for you every day. Don't forget. I mean it.'

When fate lays a baffling tragedy at your door, it can often be traced to a playful remark made years before.

But she had it wrong; she was the one who chose to run away from home, and that became the name of the coffee shop. I had the four words carved on a sign and painted white, so she couldn't miss it: Run Away From Home.

7

The area in front of the town hall was abuzz with activity. Luo Yiming had been selected as the 'Good Person–Exemplary Deeds' representative. I heard firecrackers going off before I turned at the junction. The popping sounds woke up the whole street and firecracker confetti swirled in the misty smoke above us. Some unexploded crackers were carried off by car tyres wet from the rain and lay flat in the middle of the road like discarded cigarette butts.

As well as the announcement, printed on red paper, the bulletin board also carried a sentimental narrative about Luo's accomplishments and heartfelt good wishes. A woman had probably written it, for it was filled with gratitude and sorrow. The small town rarely made it into the news, but now the bulletin board was covered with newspaper clippings, where the name Luo Yiming appeared again. Here he was, smiling broadly in photos taken at charitable events, his face lit up brightly; no one could have predicted that he would fall ill only a few years after that.

It's hard being good in today's world, and the opportunities to do good are rare, which just shows how noteworthy it was to be good like Luo Yiming, and to do good things. No wonder the town hall freed up a large space to reflect his glory, unmatched in recent years, by temporarily taking down the notices regulating vendors, resurveying marginal land and promoting electricity conservation.

It was late August, the tar turning sticky under a blistering sun, and a metallic light being constantly refracted off the gravel path in front of the shop. When there were no customers, I went out to sit under the eaves with a handful of pebbles, tossing them one at a time into a little hole I'd dug beforehand. I did that several times a day, slowly enough that each toss earned me the passing of ten seconds. I imagined the pebbles to be frogs jumping into a field, where one day they would break out into a croaking chorus and we would wake up the slumbering reeds.

The small shop stewed in the heat from the great oven overhead. Fortunately, business was slack at the time. I heard news of Luo's illness every so often, but nothing particularly bad. Once the hot summer ended, autumn would quickly show its face. The spikes on the embankment reeds grew slowly; one day they would be long enough to sway gracefully under the setting sun. Someone might walk up quietly, shielded by waves of white and carrying wind from Haikou, her hair hanging loose and her skirt fluttering. It would feel real, like a dream from which I'd just awakened.

Just when I was feeling relieved by how quickly August was moving along, time slowed down over a period of days. I found myself believing in a mysterious connection – that someone far away was writing to me. A pen was scratching away melodiously under a lamp, quietly spreading lamentations outward, as if an entire autumn had halted its approach, waiting for her, waiting for her to finish the letter, waiting for her to carefully drop it into a post box, just as the winds started up and sent bright red flame tree petals scattering to the ground.

The letter was three pages long, and was signed Luo Baixiu.

I gave it a quick glance, expecting little, and was surprised by what she wrote:

> *I changed my mind the day I was supposed to accept the award*
> *for my father. I thought I'd rather write to you, for only you*
> *know what he should do. Am I right? Only you can save him.*
> *But then I thought it over, and knew that was unlikely. If I*
> *were you, I would not be hoping he'd get better.*
> *But I'm not you, and he is, after all, my father.*

Her handwriting was small and neat, but she had pressed down too hard; the shade of ink was uneven, likely because she'd used a different pen midway through or stopped to think after each line. One thing was sure – it must have taken her a long time, for the letter was filled with weighty thoughts. But it was the following paragraph that sent a searing pain into my heart:

> *We had a lot of visitors back then, people who dropped by*
> *when Father was home for the weekend. Except for a few*
> *local friends, they were mostly businessmen. At some point,*
> *Father could no longer stand the disruptions and decided not*
> *to receive any more visitors. Only you two enjoyed special*
> *treatment. He would pace up and down the garden waiting*
> *for you to show up.*

Actually I miss her even now, an older sister to me. She was so striking she overshadowed everyone else in the room. I'm grateful to her for bringing laughter into our house, which was rare; no wonder Father liked her so much.

That must have been when the changes in his life, if that's what they were, began.

Ah, a new Miss Baixiu. What had she learned over the past couple of months that allowed me to peek into her inner world? She had finally unravelled the threads of the mystery, obviously no longer intent on holding back, instead willingly bringing up her father's emotional world.

Her reminiscences stopped abruptly, changing the subject to her father's younger sister. This aunt, who had pitched in to care for him, had her own things to attend to, so Miss Baixiu had decided to come back from Taipei to relieve her on the weekends. She continued:

I want to use this weekly opportunity – please give me a chance – to sit quietly in your shop; I promise I'll not be a pest, and you don't have to answer any foolish questions. If something really did happen, it was beyond my control at the time. So please forgive my weakness, and let me sit in front of you as a hostage.

8

And so, every Saturday afternoon since early autumn, Miss Baixiu's car has glided slowly from the bridgehead onto the gravel path in front of the shop and stopped on the grass by the building's side wall. In no hurry to get out, she sits in the driver's seat behind a windscreen speckled with swaying bamboo shadows until the last customer gets up from one of the tables and leaves.

On her first weekend visit, she walked in and, when she saw there were still customers, sat near a post to be inconspicuous, took out a book and thumbed through it in a leisurely manner, her shoulder-length hair swinging from side to side each time she checked the direction of the ocean winds as they bent the treetops. Seasonal winds lack punch in September as they speed east from Haikou, two kilometres away, and by the time they reach the stream here, they are reduced to a whisper. But Miss Baixiu had obviously not come to listen to the wind, nor did she care to focus on the book in her hands. Sitting alone, she took an occasional sip of water, small and catlike, and held it in her mouth before swallowing slowly, as if it were a weighty thought.

Over a couple of months, in order to determine when the shop was least crowded, she first showed up right after the lunch hour, when I was marking time waiting for customers; later on she delayed her arrival till three in the afternoon, after which she discreetly pushed it back to five in the evening. In recent weeks, she had obviously found the best time, and started coming in at dusk, just before dinner, when the shop was about to close.

Catching the last high-speed train out of Taipei every Friday night, then transferring to the final shuttle bus at Taichung's Wuri station must have been draining. I don't know what she could have been thinking along the way, but I imagine that the rocking trip home exhausted her, and yet she had to be ready to meet me the next day, coming to sit, as she put it, like a hostage.

Sitting quietly is in reality a form of torture for a young woman, and I suspect that she was putting herself through this meaningless ordeal in order to fulfil a vow to save her father. She showed up on time, and was in no hurry to leave even when it got late. True to the promise she had made in her letter not to be a pest, she sat quietly, like an obliging debtor who shows up at regular intervals to prove she has not run off and that she has dedicated herself to making up for past offences.

Of course, Miss Baixiu was not a debtor and she owed me nothing; it was just that she faced a predicament similar to mine, and she chose to resolve it by acting passively. She never drank my coffee, apparently as a silent reproach, and, it would seem, to show that she was not here on a romantic quest. A woman like that easily draws attention to herself, which was why, when she saw customers inside, she preferred to stay in her car under the tree, even when she was exhausted to the point of dozing off, her head slumped to one side.

Miss Baixiu, who drank only water, sometimes brought in homemade pastries, walked over to the counter for plates, and then took them back to her table, where she spread the pastries out to enjoy alone when she got hungry. Allowing herself an occasional sip of water, she chewed slowly, the absolute image of a forsaken woman. She rarely finished what was on her plate, leaving most of it, in fact, and never took what was left away with her, confident that I would most likely not throw it away, but instead, after she was gone, would quietly convert it into dinner, a simple way for a man to pass a long night.

In her eyes I must have seemed pathetic.

That was why she came with a small tin of tea leaves one weekend. After spreading a tea towel over the table and laying out the tea set, she went outside and snipped off a section of green bamboo to decorate her simple service. By then it was getting dark, and that may have created the atmosphere of solitude she was hoping for: a small coastal town, a shop plunged into total silence, she and I the only ones left, together watching steam slowly rise from a kettle on a burner.

'This way we can both take it easy,' she said.

'You really don't have to do this, Miss Baixiu.'

'Oh, I should have kept quiet.' She slid a cup of tea over to my side of the table and cast me a sorrowful look without flinching. 'Please call me Baixiu.'

Miss Baixiu . . . I paused to think that over.

'For such an upstanding family as the Luos, "Miss" is the form of address I prefer,' I told her.

She didn't respond; tears brimming in her eyes fell the moment she looked away.

I gazed out of the window at the flickering shadows in the slowly descending dusk. Bamboo leaves, disturbed by the wind, scraped across the glass panes. The noisy chirps of brambling finches, bound for their nests, brought me down a bit. Normally, I would have pulled the rolling steel door shut by this time, but for her it seemed the night was just beginning. When the gusty winds finally died out, I heard her say:

'You can put on some music.'

So I did, and then I stopped to wash some dishes at the bar as the music began to flow. I watched Miss Baixiu from behind while she poured boiling water into her teapot to warm it. I have to admit that she moved with grace and elegance, lifting the pot to just the right height and expertly adding the tea leaves. If she had been an ordinary customer who had dropped in with no particular demands of me, this could have made for a delightful evening by the sea.

Unfortunately, she not only had demands, but also, little by little, she had created an atmosphere of ingratiation. I couldn't help but be wary when I recalled the hints in her letter. Truth be told, I was no longer interested in why she had abruptly stopped talking about Qiuzi, even if she'd hoped by doing so to get me to ask about what really took place. Neither Qiuzi nor I would want anyone to casually talk about what had happened to her and to me.

I even suspected that she was cultivating some sort of relationship, one that couldn't be called love, but which she would then use to ease the tension between us. Like a hand of friendship unexpectedly offered after a fierce battle, her calm demeanour worried me, as I wondered when she might reach the limit of her forbearance; I strongly doubted that she would remain in a supplicating mode for long. When the time came, she could well get up and say, through tears of sadness, 'Look, I've done everything that's required of a hostage. What else do you want? Why don't you close up shop and go away from here?'

Pastries do not come without cost, and neither does tea.

She asked me a strange question that night, just before our little tea ceremony was over: 'Do you have any religious beliefs?'

I shook my head and told her I'd once had faith in everyone.

'Ai—' Her voice brimmed with affection. 'No wonder you can't get over it.'

'I'm doing all right. Actually, there was no need for you to come again.'

'No,' she said, 'I have to find a way to revive your soul.'

9

Miss Baixiu, who wanted to revive my soul, dozed off in her car.

After I had had only two stragglers all day long, a group visiting the wetland swarmed in at dusk on their way home and took up all the space in the café. Among them were a few young teachers, each carrying a camera that must have been filled with pictures of terns, teals and fiddler crabs. Their laughter carried a hint of aggression from too much excitement, as they showered me with questions about the café: *How many cups do you sell a day? Do you have customers at night? What a surprise to find something like this here . . .*

After the group finished and walked out, I was pulling down the rolling door when I realized that Miss Baixiu should be here on one of her weekend visits. I snatched a quick look, and sure enough, the rear end of her white car was peeking out from under the tree. Awakened by the sound of the closing door, she hurried out of the car, skipped over and ducked in underneath.

I was stunned by the Miss Baixiu who walked in. A pair of

thighs under a short skirt invaded my field of vision; her snowy white knees seemed to be talking to me. That glance alone told me that her skirt was too short; I even suspected she might be hitching it up, except her arms were crossed in front of her chest, as if she were cold.

So I turned my gaze to her face, which retained a rosy glow from the nap. Her forehead, on the other hand, seemed unusually bright. She'd had a haircut, and not just a trim; her long hair had been sheared off all the way to just below her earlobes. Her neck, which the long hair had obscured, was suddenly uncovered to display a snowy whiteness.

The new Miss Baixiu mystified me.

Granted, she was entitled to her freedom, not to mention the fact that my standards were never precise. My concept of beauty was usually based on my feelings of the moment; to me, what was bewitching often reflected homeliness, while an impressive degree of ugliness could embody beauty. I wasn't concerned about her looks, nor did I find the length of her skirt problematic. Women stroll down the streets all the time with their underwear peeking out from their skirts when they bend over, and shapeless long skirts like the one she'd worn that first day didn't necessarily convey elegance. Beauty resides in what is appropriate. In fact, there was nothing indecent in the short skirt she was wearing this evening. But she hadn't dressed like that before, and that was a surprise. A woman who normally wears long skirts can look refreshing and radiant when she exposes her thighs, but for her to appear in front of me like that felt inappropriate.

The curious sight of her back as she busied herself with something at the sink truly made me feel like grumbling. Speaking of short skirts, there are plenty of women who shiver with quivering legs in the cold; they have misunderstood what it takes to be beautiful. If nudity evokes the image of a discarded body, then why not cover it up instead? The same goes for short hair, which does not work for all women. Some wear it short to achieve a bright, sunny appearance, while others shear off their long hair over disappointment in love. But for someone like Miss Baixiu, who showed up with her hair cut short for no obvious reason, I wondered why she'd done that to herself, other than to mock me.

Qiuzi looked natural in short hair, a style she'd adopted when we first met. It was never longer than chin length, layered to a tapered end, like a fox gazing at snow on the nape of her neck. She had a small face, a tall, slender figure, and a voice like a bird's chirrups. If that Qiuzi had suddenly decided to let her hair grow, she could have looked more polished, however difficult that might have been to pull off, but sooner or later, she would have been frightened by her own staccato way of speaking.

I certainly hoped my view of Miss Baixiu was just a mistaken impression on my part. For herself, she seemed quite pleased with the change, her smiling eyes revealing her feelings. When she walked over after drying her hands at the sink, the corners of her mouth were upturned, and she didn't try to avoid my eyes, as she had done before.

Without question, she had turned up in a whole new body, head to toe.

And that annoyed me. Why did she have to cut her hair in the style of Qiuzi?

'You must be filled with anticipation,' she said.

She walked up and moved two tables to the side, and then backed off to consider the arrangement. After making some adjustments, she produced a folded piece of old-fashioned indigo fabric and shook it out. Its upper-right corner was decorated with dots of grey dye resembling the silhouette of a plum flower.

Before reviving my soul, she wanted first to conjure a dove out of the fabric, it seemed.

I laughed silently, reminded of her sorry appearance as she'd run in from the rain that day, and of the offer she'd made in her letter to be my hostage. But now, at this instant, this very moment, on this evening, after I'd been in town for more than six months, she discovered that I had lost my soul and that she needed to revive it with a piece of fabric.

After spreading the printed cloth over the table, she pointed to the half-open door. I knew what she meant. It was dark outside, and a crescent moon was faintly visible in the east, while the area around Haikou was overcast in dim desolation. The light inside deepened after I pulled the door all the way down, shutting out the noise coming from the stream.

'Shut the window and draw the curtains.'

I did as she said, and asked her if she needed music.

'That won't be necessary,' she said.

'I have to tell you, I don't have any candles, just in case you want to perform witchcraft.'

She blinked but didn't respond, as she waited for me to take a seat.

I couldn't stare at her the whole time, so I turned to the door, to my invisible back in the loft, and to the small potted plants from early summer, when I had first opened for business. My mood plummeted, as always, when my eyes fell upon these absurd objects.

Luckily, the gentle Miss Baixiu understood, for she leaned forward and said with a faint smile:

'It's all right. We don't have to start if you're not ready.'

II

I seemed to be talking in my own dream

Cadillac, the black flagship of my dreams, a monstrous luxury sedan, took me on an inspection tour, as though we were on a cruise. The driver had lowered the lacy white curtain behind the front seats, instantly transforming the back into a private space. All was quiet around me, except for the noisy thumping of my heart. I was sitting in a private box, feeling like a thief who has just made a successful grab.

As I drew the window shades apart, I saw orange flags with emblems on the front wings. A spring breeze under a radiant, warm sun felt as implausible as a dreamland. It was usually at moments like this that I recalled an image of my father pinned down in an extremely gloomy corner and unable to get out. I wish he could be sitting beside me having just kicked off his rubber boots, even if only briefly, so he could enjoy the sensation of sweat on his forehead as it turns into flowing music. I would ask the driver to slow down; we were in no hurry, while Father had little time left.

I never knew what he was thinking that night. Why had he turned his bicycle around and headed for the water, icy cold as it was in late January? Most of the village women had long since stopped going there to wash clothes, while he sank to the bottom to keep warm, leaving me to grieve with my arms around Mother.

1

Ah, Miss Baixiu, our consciousness as humans must have begun when we were but infants. A pair of sneakers can create our first happy memory, and our aspirations often begin with our love for someone. Over time, all but a very few people will have encountered myriad life experiences.

But what is a soul? Miss Baixiu, how are you going to revive mine? You'd have to have been there when I was eight to witness my childhood – it was early morning and I'd already put on my shoes. Come and revive me. I was about to set out and confront a life experience that would be a mixture of happiness and sorrow.

I'd laced the shoes myself before looping my book bag around my neck. Oh, how I was looking forward to my first day at school! With the sun scaling up to the eaves, I dragged Father out anxiously, forcing him to put down his bowl and leave my half-fed mother on the muddy floor.

He let go of my hand when we reached the street.

'Hey, let's run from here.'

But I didn't want to soil my new uniform with sweat, despite my eagerness to get to school.

'Well then, we'll run for a short distance and stop to walk before we reach the gate.'

That sounded good, so I took off running and quickly left him behind.

Now that I think back, I realize that he'd also been in a hurry that day. He worked at the school I was starting that day. I felt none of a new student's shyness or resistance; all I wanted was to find my classroom and sit down, because I was proud of him. He was free to come and go anywhere on the campus, and no one would ever try to stop him.

Droves of parents were standing outside the school gate, where staff members eagerly showed them where to register. Just as we were a few steps from the gate, someone from a higher grade called out in a peculiar voice:

'You're late today, Old Zhang.'

Father snickered, but didn't respond. I was pleased though – someone recognized him, even from a distance, which could only mean that he was a prominent figure. People don't necessarily know the name of a postman, for example – whether it's Lao Zhang or Lao Huang – even though he delivers mail on his bicycle all day long.

He vanished after handing me over to my teacher. When the bell rang at the end of the first period, I stood in the hallway waiting for him. He didn't return. He also failed to show up when the second period ended. Though I was disappointed, I knew he would be busy on the first day of school, if not with administrative duties, then with more important work. Otherwise, he wouldn't have left me like that without a word.

I stayed outside the classroom when the last period started. Hugging the wall so I wouldn't be seen, I stood on my tiptoes to check every room with a window, but he wasn't in any of them. I kept looking for him until I reached the principal's office, where the sign on the wall raised goosebumps on my arms. I actually thought I'd finally found him, and yet that seemed too good to be true. Suddenly overcome by my elevated image of him, I felt my heart race.

The principal turned out to be an old woman whose glasses hung down over her chest on a chain that swayed as her hands moved.

The following scene in my memory is of Father, in black rubber overalls and clunky rubber boots, squatting by a stove in a tin-roofed room in order to scrub the filthy floor. Beside him along the wall is a row of boilers. Bottles of oil, vinegar and other condiments sit on a tiled counter alongside piles of vegetables. A wave of heat comes in through the kitchen door. A ventilation pump whirrs loudly through two openings at the far end. He is holding a red plastic brush in both hands to scrub the floor, after which he rinses it with water before repeating the process. With the sound of scrubbing absorbed by the pump and his eyes focused on the red brush, he doesn't sense my presence behind him the whole time.

Instead of calling out, I quietly left the tin-roofed room and waited until the last bell to join a group of students walking home. Mother was still sitting on the floor, having moved inside on her own. I wiped the saliva off her chin, but she was so happy to see me that she drooled even more.

When he returned, Father asked me how the classes went, whether I was all right with school, and if I'd made any new friends. I rattled off a few names, of neighbourhood playmates, my first ever lie. He didn't react to the deception, but neither did he respond.

Over the next three years, we never again walked to school together. I went through the same routine every morning, finding an excuse to duck into the toilet or rearrange my bag so he could leave without me. I'd then follow by turning into an alley and dashing onto the main street before racing through side streets that criss-crossed like a chessboard and finally entering school through the rear gate.

The landlord took the house back when I was in the fourth grade, so we moved even farther away from school into a house that was more dilapidated than the previous one. To my delight, there was a long, narrow empty plot in front of the house, and a fence topped with loofah gourd vines, which were in bloom at the time, drawing swarms of bees. Alerted by the bees' presence, dragonflies flitted over from the wild, and sometimes sparrows too. Many insects whose names I didn't know built nests in mounds of dirt. Finally Mother had things to talk to during the day, her throaty mumbling slowly turning airy and melodious.

With school farther away, I had to ride in with Father on a rickety bicycle someone had given him. I rode sideways so I could jump off when we went up a slope beyond the tilled field. The trip took about half an hour, during which we rarely spoke. He usually stopped at the earth god temple near the school gate and had me offer respects with him. When I was done, he told me to go on to school while he stayed behind to talk to the earth god.

Before the term was half over that year, someone ran off with the money from the savings club Father had started, and club members kept coming to school demanding their money back. Some of them lodged complaints with the principal, while others watched my father kneel on the ground and beg for more time. I came upon many of these unbearable scenes, but I hid and watched him in secret, just as I had the time I'd learned of his low standing as the school caretaker.

We began having visitors the following spring, usually around dinnertime. When there were enough of them, they shut the door leading to an empty room behind the stove and played cards. Keeping an eye on me as I did my homework, Father made hourly trips to pour more tea and clean the ashtrays. Around midnight, he had to go and buy snacks and drinks, sometimes returning with a big bag of sweets that he quietly left on my bed.

I'd watched those men sitting around a table, each with money in front of him. There was more money in the centre, which the winner swept into his own pile when the last card was flipped over, and handed Father some loose change. Thus began my basic understanding of money, for it enabled Father to purchase a multi-geared bicycle and even get Mother into hospital for three days. We also bought our first TV set. In April of that year, a ferryboat sank in Su'ao, drowning three dozen college students and their teachers, which led to the resignation of Chiang Yen-shih, the Minister of Education, as I recall.

The powerful minister lost his power, while my powerless father tried to restart his life by facilitating illegal gambling. By then my adulation of power had begun to waver, and I realized that money was more important than anything else. It bought all kinds of medication and created a miracle for Mother, who could now mend my socks, though her fingers were still clumsy. I jumped up and down and happily wept as she bit off the thread when she was done.

An understanding of money formed in my head. If we had some, Old Zhang wouldn't have to scrub the floor at school. And maybe Mother wouldn't always be sitting on the floor at home. After mulling over these thoughts, I eventually concluded that I could do something to help out, especially if I quietly earned money while I was asleep. Wouldn't it be great not to waste time during my long sleeping hours?

That was how the little goat came to live in a pen next to our house. It was black, with a grey ring around its neck. It bleated in a raspy voice, as if it was still adjusting to its new environment, sort of like the way I finally got used to school life by my fifth year.

The first thing I did each morning after getting up was go to the pen to look at the goat and rub its head. It was maturing more slowly than I'd hoped, but it was the first wish I had as I grew up, and it embodied my resentment and concessions towards Father. I was quietly waiting for the goat to grow up so I could give it to him.

I'd shared part of this story with Qiuzi, but didn't have time to tell her how it ended. Apart from that, I rarely talked about my parents, for I'd thought love meant to hold back, out of good intentions, and I hadn't wanted her to hear about too much sadness. But I'd been wrong, and now it was too late. If I hadn't hidden these things from her, but instead had supplied her with an appropriate dose of sorrow's magical power, she might have thought twice about leaving when she encountered a setback.

She was unaware of what happened next. Our goat seemed to have gone mad, its cries waking me up in the middle of the night. The police were pounding on our door and eventually broke it down. The gamblers and their money were whisked away to the police station. A few days later, my father was fired from his janitorial job, forcing us into a tight spot. Our life took a turn for the worse, as did Mother's health. Yellow flowers continued to bloom on the loofah gourd vines, still drawing swarms of bees, but winter came before we knew it. Early one morning that winter, Father quietly floated to the surface in the deep water of a local stream.

2

I spent ten months at a military base called Yongchunpo on Taipei's Songshan Road, waiting to be discharged after returning with my offshore unit. That was before I met Qiuzi; or, in other words, I had not known that in this wide world a woman named Qiuzi would soon enter my life. Every Sunday morning, after finishing a breakfast of steamed buns, I took a city bus from Songshan Road to Ximending, where I had my first real taste of a city. I walked around aimlessly all day in civilian clothes. Late in the afternoon before my leave ended, I stopped at book shops along Chongqing South Road and then strolled over to a street corner to wait under an overhang for a bus to take me back to the base.

That was the only Taipei I knew, bustling and filled with opportunities, nothing like my bleak hometown or my military base on the island of Mazu, surrounded by a vast, hazy ocean. The prosperous city brought me an unfamiliar sense of happiness. I believed I would someday become one of its residents.

I couldn't have been more mistaken. A soldier decommissioned at the same time as I was let me stay at his house for a while. I wrote and sent out a dozen application letters, but didn't receive a single response. As I perused the 'help wanted' ads in the newspaper, I concentrated on clerical jobs, which for a young, immature ex-soldier like me seemed like a fairly pragmatic way to start. But Taipei wasn't generous enough to give me even a modest little bit of its sky.

Ten days into my job search, I was on the evening bus back to my temporary lodging when we made a detour and stopped at a junction where one of the streets, Zhongxiao East Road, was unnaturally dark and gloomy. I spotted a dark mass of people lying in the street. Affected by what was an unknown sadness, I didn't hesitate to act. I got off the bus and lay down. The strangers around me were older than me. I thought they must have suffered just like I had done and, instead of going home, had decided to lie down in the street.

'Why are you here?' a bearded man turned to ask me.

'Um, I don't know. I just got out of the military.'

'You must be desperate too. Getting married soon, I suppose.'

In the half hour that followed, I learned that this was the sensational Shell-less Snail Movement. Many people took turns shouting through a hand-held megaphone, protesting against the government's failure to implement its housing policy, as soaring prices chased young people out of Taipei even though they wanted to settle there. I realized I'd lain down for the wrong cause. Looking at the cheerless, overcast evening sky, I thought of Mother, who, with help from neighbours, had been placed in an adult care centre. I myself no longer had a physical house or an actual home to return to.

I left Taipei the next day.

Mother died soon after I went to visit her, having

tenaciously held on to see me one last time before shutting her eyes. From the expression in those eyes, I was convinced that her mind could not have been clearer than it was at that moment. As I held her hand, her twisted face relaxed as if an electric current had flowed through it, the lines slowly dispersing like rippling water; her sallow skin turned red and then white, two colours that looked beautiful on her.

Three months after her death, I walked into the general manager's office at a construction company. My nearly blank résumé lay on his desk. He asked what had emboldened me to apply, since I had no work experience. I stressed to him that I had come prepared, reciting a long list of book titles that dealt with advertising. But he wasn't listening; instead, he randomly chose a sheet from the handful of topics in his hand.

On the blank sheet was a single short line:

The Hilton is not on Kenan Street

I knew about the Hilton, a big Taipei hotel whose fancy sign had greeted me each time I passed by Zhongxiao West Road. But where was Kenan Street? The Taipei I knew had only Songshan Road and Ximending. Yet I could guess what was going on. I imagined that they were planning on pre-selling a housing development on Kenan Street in some city. It might not be called Hilton, but they aspired to a high-quality product on the scale of the Hilton.

Wary that Kenan Street, a place I didn't know, might hide something that could trip me up, I decided not to take a risk.

So I asked for a different topic, trying my best to explain my lack of familiarity with the geographical surroundings. After casting me a pitying look, the general manager leafed through the sheets. He was a good man. Heavyset with short arms, he looked as if he was trying to select a providential gift for me. Fifteen years later, I would hop into a taxi to see him sitting behind the steering wheel, his hair much thinner, his grey woollen waistcoat turning fuzzy from wear.

In the end, he gave me a reverse question, a narrative for me to come up with a caption.

It was a tired narrative about a family searching high and low but failing to find their dream house in a market inundated with slipshod structures, until they happen upon . . .

The lack of ingenuity put my mind at ease. So that's what property ads are all about, I thought, certainly not beyond my ability to handle. No longer worried, I didn't hurry to finish it and hand it back to him promptly; instead, I scanned the shop signs outside his window in search of inspiration.

Yet at that precise moment on a summer morning eight days after my mother's death, something puzzling happened to me, and I found myself spiralling into a daze, perhaps due to extreme sorrow. Nothing came to me as time passed slowly. I remember laying the ballpoint pen sideways on the paper. I wondered what kind of sadness was behind my odd mood, and, inexplicably, recalled the shadowy figures lying on Zhongxiao East Road that night and the sight of my father rushing onto the campus after I'd gone in the school gate. And with that came the realization that I had nothing left. Besieged by all these inopportune thoughts and emotions, not only did I fail to write a single word on the paper, but tears breached my eyes and began to stream down my cheeks.

I forget how I finally managed to produce the caption. When I thought about it later, I supposed that the GM had been sympathetic and, after sensing enormous energy emanating from my sorrow, believed I could turn out to be some sort of genius. The tears were not shed in vain. He frowned as he read the lines I had scribbled, but offered me a generous three-month trial period.

That marked my entry into the world of property, as I was assigned to the company's planning department, where my senior colleagues, all women, had unmatched skill in sketching and were fast and accurate in their art designs. I was a different kettle of fish, forced to tap a hole in my head in search of an idea.

I found the ideas that surfaced supremely attractive, for they came from an imaginary space of unbridled freedom, which suited a marginal figure like me perfectly, someone with nothing to his name. More importantly, I found a powerful appeal in the field of advertising, where I was allowed to say what I wanted and venture into other people's minds; I could speak not just to total strangers, but also to myself. The idea of power no longer baffled me, and maybe a pen could showcase my ability to come and go as I pleased.

Admittedly, the heavens had other plans for me. By this time, in fact, I was already walking in a city where Qiuzi was about to appear. Nothing presaged it, but I was filled with joy for no apparent reason. I went to work with a smile each day and received praise for every assignment I completed as a result of torturous effort. I'm not sure, but maybe Qiuzi had something to do with that. When the woman I would come to love deeply was about to appear, everything seemed to show off its finest, its original beauty; I was surrounded by a serene elegance, and the weather was unusually cool and comfortable, like a forest that gave off a freshness that ceaselessly infused my sweet dreams.

3

You see, Miss Baixiu, I was doing quite well at the time. I lived alone in a rented apartment and took care of my own meals, with nothing to tie me down. I was about to set sail on a beautiful life. I was just waiting for a woman to enter my world and become the first addition to my family.

Where is my soul? Ah, let me help you find it. At the very least, its owner had a completely unfettered body back then, and was no longer chained to a desk; even a light drizzle was enough of an excuse for him to stay at home, and he could sleep until noon after staying up late into the night. Sometimes at a matinee showing at the cinema, he stayed in his seat to enjoy the soundtrack during the credits. You should know that he had become an orphan almost overnight, and that loneliness gripped him only when he was homesick. That's not a bad thing, since some people are lonely even when they don't miss home. His loneliness was a luxury with a price tag. It was a wonderful world, and he told himself he mustn't waste what time he had left.

I do my best not to miss home, Miss Baixiu. You can see

that if I had a family, say with Qiuzi when she finally appeared, I'd protect her with my life. How could I have let her leave for no reason? But of course, it was too early to think of that. I had no idea where she was or what she looked like, not to mention the fact that your father had yet to show up in my world too. So treat this as someone else's story and listen as you please. The soul is not an easy thing to pin down. If you find it at some point in this tale of my life, tell me to stop right there, or otherwise just wait till I finish to draw your own conclusion. Or think of it as me talking in my dreams and just watch from a distance. Even if you do see my soul, you will realize that it is a despicable one.

But don't think I lived an idle, footloose life back then. I was conscientious and devoted to my work. If I sensed an imminent visit from the muse, I immediately tensed up. Even during a tempestuous rainstorm or after I'd been up till dawn, I'd hop on my motor scooter and, carrying the fruit of my latest inspiration with me, race to the office, arriving there before I could feel I was truly alive. I jumped to my feet during a romantic scene in a film one night simply because of being struck by an idea, and stormed out of the cinema intent on finding the quickest route to somewhere. An iridescent moon shone in my eyes, but in my head there was a clear blue sky. I felt like running, or better yet, flying down streets like the wind whipping through the treetops.

Pay attention, Miss Baixiu. It's time for Qiuzi to make her appearance.

One day, I had yet another incredible idea, this time at a jam and conserve shop tucked away on a side street. I'd just picked out two jars of strawberry jam and hadn't yet paid for them. A barely perceptible but profound premonition had found its way into my head. Knowing what was happening, I quietly put the jam down and practically tiptoed to the door, taking pains to act nonchalant, for I was afraid the shape of the idea would shift amid my excitement, since it was still barely perceptible, flitting through my mind for a brief but sweet moment.

It was around three o'clock that afternoon, as summer was giving way to the autumn of 1995. I walked a hundred metres east and found a coffee shop where a small table by the inside wall sat empty, as if it had been reserved for me. Obviously, I wasn't aware that Qiuzi was in there. But if she hadn't been, life might as well not have existed for me. Naturally, though, I didn't appreciate the full impact of this day until much later, after I'd given it lots of thought. As you walk down the road of happiness or sorrow, it can take years to sort out what to remember and what to forget.

I'd never had coffee at this shop, which wasn't easy to spot, what with its shabby eaves and a doorway all but blocked by motor scooters. If not for the serendipitous desire to buy two jars of jam, I would likely not have walked in, but instead would have gone straight home to my rented flat.

But I did walk in.

Quietly taking out pen and paper, with a reverential seriousness I wrote down the caption that had formed in my head, not letting a single word escape my full attention. I couldn't control my greedy pen when that was done, and wonderful thoughts continued to pour out of it; soon I had a complete ad, one that was nearly perfect.

Finally, I was able to relax and enjoy a cigarette, my ears attuned to the lovely music flowing softly around me and to a water feature murmuring amid indoor plants. Everything took on such a pleasant aura that even the laughter and loud talk coming from nearby tables sounded like the emotive waves of a symphonic movement.

Half an hour later, a loud banging noise erupted from the table across from mine. I saw that it was a group of girls who were knocking on the tabletop, and a dozen eyes glared at me from that direction before the girls got up to leave. It was a protest, probably against the cigarette in my hand. A cloud of white smoke hung in the air.

The girls scowled as they passed my table on the way to the counter.

I waved at the last of their group, who was walking more slowly than the others; her face turned bright red.

'I wasn't doing it,' she said.

I pointed at a paper bag on the sofa, to which she replied with a shake of her head, 'It's empty.'

But she turned back anyway and picked it up.

Her eyes shone brightly under long lashes that shielded single-fold lids on a bashful face. She had a pouty look when she spoke, scrunching up a little mole in protest. I could tell she was angry with herself for speaking to me; I looked at her without saying anything. She passed by, chin up, after retrieving the bag. Her annoyance was clearly not caused by my cigarette, but by an interaction that put her at a distinct disadvantage. Her shoes clacked angrily as she walked out.

She and I would have missed each other for ever if I'd continued to smoke or if a sudden rain shower had not hit at that moment. But ten minutes after that encounter, I gathered up my draft and walked out, spotting the girls huddled together under a small awning, the angry one on the outside, her chest nearly pressed up against her friend's back. Rain splashed down on her pale neck, which took on a sheen under her short hair.

There was no room for even another foot under the awning. She shivered as she glanced at me. Seconds later, she moved further in and held her hand behind her back to beckon me with her pinkie, as if we were a family taking shelter from the rain, and she had to find a way to pull me in. I was startled by the simple gesture; it would have been unseemly for me to move over to them, but I felt an urge to know more about her. I couldn't tell if she felt the same, but the kindness of a stranger tugged on my heart, which had been lonely for a long time.

I didn't know how to let her know what was on my mind. Sooner or later, the rain would stop and the sky would clear up. What would I do if the girls abruptly broke up and went their separate ways? Without thinking, I took out a business card and, while she was still holding the bag, tossed it in through the opening, as though I was dropping off a letter.

I believed she'd noticed something white flash past her eyes, for she looked surprised. She turned her head, but then hesitated and lowered it before our eyes met.

She finally called three months later.

'I fretted over the card,' she said. 'I remembered it because it rained that day.'

'I thought you must have thrown the bag away along with the card.'

'I knew there was a card in it, so I kept the bag.'

She was a waitress at a French restaurant. Her family called her Qiuzi, Autumn Child, since that was when she'd been born.

Mobile phones weren't so ubiquitous then, and the extension number she gave me for her apartment was a pain, as the superintendent would cut the connection after only a few rings. One day I decided to watch her through the window of her restaurant. Dressed in black velvet trousers, with a red waistcoat over a white shirt, she circled the tables holding a round tray, bent at a thirty-degree angle when talking to diners. Flickering candles beneath a crystal chandelier cast shadows on the linen tablecloths. She smiled bashfully and squinted under the diners' gazes.

We finally met again when winter arrived. She was preparing for a routine assessment at work, so she recited a string of names for me: Giuliano Tartufi sea salt, some German herbal salt, Himalayan rock salt, Maldon smoked sea salt, Guérande truffle salt, Carmen Valencia sea salt, French fleur de sel, and so on, as if her restaurant sold only salt.

The Qiuzi I got to know probably originated with this salt list recitation. Reciting the names of salt fit her perfectly, as the words were odd but not too long, like her brief utterances, as though she had trouble managing a complete sentence. I imagined girls like her to be forthright, with no strange ideas hidden in their clear, simple vocabulary. Her standard remarks when we met were: want to be an assistant head of staff; outrageous; living in Nantou County; deep in the mountains; lend me a book; so you're in advertising; someone's coming this way.

The property market was still booming, rewarding agents with bulging red bonus envelopes, while my salary, however steady, barely filled my trouser pocket. I didn't envy those estate agents, and yet their elated expressions made me keenly aware of my impoverished state. I would, if I could, splurge on a nice outfit and walk elegantly into the restaurant during her shift to have her come up to me with her tray, drape a clean white napkin over my lap, and, with bright, shining eyes, take my order.

The next time we met, she was going through a year-end assessment, this time with a focus on food. She went through the menu for me, vicariously warming my stomach on a cold winter night: *scallop appetizer, followed by escargot, and as a side dish, Yilan duck brought in just that morning. Oh, right, and Mengzong bamboo. Can you believe it?*

'I have dug Mengzong bamboo,' she said. 'It has to be done before dawn, when the ground is dew covered. You must carefully push the leaves away and check the mark in the soil; if you see the tip you're too late.'

'We planted loofah gourds when I was a child. A bumper crop always troubled me . . .'

I stopped abruptly, surprised by a tiny gesture that she made: she tucked her sleeve into her palm, raised her hand, and held it in front of her mouth.

I asked her what was wrong. It turned out the gesture meant: 'Tell me, first tell me why you were troubled.'

'Because there were so many gourds I didn't know which to eat first.'

That was all it took to make her laugh. I noticed that her happiness was always tinged with a sense of wonder and that she laughed a little too early. The hint of a smile would dance around her lips when I was only partway through telling her something; it gave her a foolish look, but I really liked how artless she was.

It was probably too soon to say I'd fallen for her; more likely, I was just curious. I wondered how, given her inexperience and untainted nature, she would deal with what life held in store for her. If she happened to hear even a snippet of my weighty past, would that dimple still dance along with her smile?

Maybe she smiled like that because she was born to give me a small dose of tenderness whenever I needed it.

'Where was I?' she asked.

'You're having an assessment at the restaurant. You were talking about Mengzong bamboo.'

'Outrageous.' Her expression turned serious as she resumed her recitation, but this time to herself.

4

A person can fall in love several times in a lifetime, but I'd still preferred to do so only once. That is, I already knew that there was nothing more on the horizon, even though I had only just started out on the road to my first romance. My certainty might seem absurd to some, but who can tell which romance turns out to be the right one? Love is elusive, like a flash of inspiration, without which our minds are nothing but a dead sea. Only when waves surge in one's mind is one able to appreciate how a lonely world can turn around. Seize the moment, and you will have gained what you need to turn away from the ripples after the waves flatten out; you can tie the ship up when it is time to go ashore.

Qiuzi was that moment, a most pleasantly surprising inspiration.

That year she was ten years younger than me, just as I would still be ten years her senior fifty years later. Differences of the heart, however, cannot be accounted for in this way. Such differences wouldn't be obvious when we were older, but they were quite significant at this early stage of our lives. She seemed too young, immature, like her family's Mengzong bamboo, which had yet to break the surface of the ground, while I had inherited so much sorrow that I easily wallowed in anxiety. Simply put, I was eager to add a member to my family of one, whereas she was down on the ground playing like the little girl next door; I was worried that I would be waiting at the finishing line while she was encountering the first obstacles in her life's journey.

And so, panicking over the possibility that I might be too late, I quit my steady, carefree job in the winter of that year and became a salesman for houses that were yet to be built. I decided to challenge my solemn, inarticulate nature, in the hope that Qiuzi would no longer have to recite the names of salts.

Qiuzi mattered more than any difficulties.

I began travelling all over Taiwan on my motor scooter, tracking clients in remote towns and isolated villages. The farthest spot I visited was a place called Muguakeng, where I skidded on a county road and wound up in an irrigation ditch. Injuries to my body would heal at some point, and setbacks at work could be reversed, as long as I got past the pivotal moment.

There was one type of wound, however, that I couldn't battle through. When my dejection came, it usually brought on dark clouds that made me feel even worse. Father became a number of apparitions. I couldn't see him up in the sky, nor could I make out the locale of his wandering soul, but I knew he could appear in my solitude at any moment, his face bloated and pale. No wonder the woman by the river had wrapped her arms around me to stop me from looking that morning.

I had been doing well enough, enduring little suffering in my solitary life, and he had few opportunities to appear because I refused to think about him. My sense of solitude began to change after meeting Qiuzi, though. I thought about her all the time, constantly besieged by emptiness and confusion, which provided him with an opening to sneak in. In one way, his presence could be a comfort, but truly he cast me into even deeper sorrow.

I never told Qiuzi about this.

Three months after we met, on the afternoon I finally got my bonus, I went to the restaurant without telling her ahead of time. The chandelier had been turned on, but diners had yet to arrive at the elegantly laid tables. The staff were standing at the entrance listening to a man, their boss, who was likely quizzing them on rules of service. I pressed my face up against the window for a closer look, afraid that Qiuzi might be singled out for mistakes – for forgetting to clean the toilet or for missing the Carmen Valencia or some such salt. In any case, I was worried about her; I felt anxious, as though I was trying to swallow with a dry mouth. I had forgotten that I was there to celebrate with a pocket full of money; I had been hoping to sit at her table and be her first customer of the night.

The stream of cars behind honked at me, so I moved from one window to the next, my feet straddling the lines between parking spaces. The night's diners filed inside. Their murmured conversations were faint from where I stood. Well decked out, they looked so elegant, and I remembered, suddenly, that I was still wearing company clothes. Mud clung to my shoes and, most importantly, I'd neglected to wash at work before heading there. There was no absolute requirement to wash your face before dining in a restaurant that served western food, and I hated French restaurants, where diners were expected to shower first and wear perfume. I would be smiling with a dirty face, which would embarrass Qiuzi, and she would be tense when she draped the napkin over my lap, because she would also see a button missing on my company shirt.

Besides, I wouldn't want to be just another diner gawping at her.

What a shame, I said to myself. I'd rushed over with the bonus so as not to let my burning sense of excitement cool. Being in love means you want the other person to learn your good news right away. Joy is heightened when it is shared at the earliest possible moment. I had wasted a pleasant surprise.

I ended up having a bowl of rice with a braised pig's knuckle in a nearby covered passageway and then went to a book shop to wait for her to get off work.

The urge to share my good news with her vanished as Qiuzi told me about the day's assessment, which she'd hoped would get her a promotion to assistant manager. Given anyway to speaking in short phrases, now she sounded short of breath, and I tensed up as her words hit my ear. I had thought the promotion was assured, but she abruptly swallowed and took a breath to say:

'I didn't make it.'

'How can that be? You sounded so smooth when you recited it for me.'

'There's also the technical stuff.'

I laughed until I was nearly crying. Who'd ever heard of technical stuff in an assessment of restaurant staff? She told me that the manager had acted as if he was a customer watching her serve the food and listening to her detailed explanation of every dish.

'I had a line ready and practised it for a long time. I didn't leave out a single word.'

'Let's hear it.'

'I know there's room for improvement, so please be frank.'

'What do you mean? Were you required to say that?'

'No, I added it. I thought I could score points, but instead, points were deducted. He said I should have used my head and not said anything about improvement before I'd even served the food.'

'But the rest was all right, wasn't it?'

'I did well with the dishes. That was my favourite part. It was like *I* was about to dine.'

'Then you should have passed the test.'

'I forgot to brush away the breadcrumbs. It was outrageous. He littered the table with them.'

I timed her roughly; she didn't smile for ten minutes, and her dimple was nowhere in sight. That dimple didn't lie; like me, it was disconsolate any time she was.

He dropped those crumbs on purpose! She was still grumbling an hour later.

5

By the end of the third year at my new job, I had started spending nights in the model house at the construction site. Nearby there was a temple whose soaring eaves were visible from my window and from which sutra recitations drifted across. Any potential buyer who heard them would leave without a word after viewing the scale models.

It was a site most people avoided, but one I had plenty of opportunities to learn more about.

I enjoyed the brimming vitality of the place at daybreak and got to watch new construction take shape, step by step, starting with draining off the water. Soon backhoes came to excavate, while workers waited to bundle steel rods and move the foundation work to the preliminary stage of pouring concrete. Though it seemed to progress slowly, the foundation work was in fact the minute-by-minute creation of an actual life form, an embryonic growth one could miss by not paying attention. Workers surrounded the bundled rods with wooden frames each day as trucks brought in more materials. A woman selling betel nuts arrived in her ankle boots and wandered around in the steel forest. Then the frames around the bundles of rods went up, followed by the walls. Plumbing and electrical inspections were conducted and approvals were given after each one. Cement mixers came and went, and when the rising columns of dust settled, the melodious sutras once again drifted over from the temple.

While the structure was rising up out of the ground, my sales targets remained six feet under.

Once a week I attended a master class in selling property. The class was jam-packed; shadowy figures turned it into a crowded train carriage ready to embark on its journey to an economic miracle. The event lacked only a bugle sounding a call to arms from the lecturer, who wore the red sash bestowed on the top agent. In addition to writing on a whiteboard, he sometimes picked out the most frequent attendees for role-playing in order to demonstrate a variety of sales scenarios.

He gave us an example that illustrated why he was awarded the title of top agent every year.

'Let's say a client hesitates and wants to ask the gods for instruction – hey, that's your opening. When he returns, don't worry if half the gods he queried were opposed to the purchase. Tell him to go back and cast the *zhijiao*, what we call *buei*. It's okay if the two crescents both land face up. Ask him whose name he used when he cast the tallies. There are all sorts of reasons for him to cast again, and eventually they'll land the way you want. But if luck isn't with you, there's still one more trick you can use. You have enough wiggle room in the selling price that you lower it a bit and tell him to go and cast one more time. Maybe that will be the price the gods are waiting to hear.'

He was literally foaming at the mouth. More bubbles gathered and, at the right time, he sucked half of the foam back in, leaving the rest to build up to the next crest. At one point, he solemnly announced a piece of good news: a public construction company had made available to him a few management positions, and those who received the top test scores at the end of the lecture series would . . .

Energized, the attendees laughed as they took notes. Among us were a retired military officer and a direct sales representative who had earned blue-diamond status, as well as a disaffected white-collar worker who hoped to turn his life around by changing jobs. One attendee who had given up his breakfast diner told me that his family had to have a house they could call their own.

I wanted to comfort him by saying that I didn't even have a family, but in the end I held back.

Time went by, and one morning in late autumn, when I was left with no choice, I finally told my first lie.

The client was an old woman who wanted to buy a place for her son's widow. She had been thinking it over for two weeks before making an appointment. On this day her daughter-in-law came with her to look at the show home. Finally, they settled on the smallest one and went home to collect a down payment before signing the contract.

I hadn't expected them to make a detour into the neighbourhood temple on their way home.

'I'm sorry,' the old woman told me over the phone. 'I cast the tallies and they both landed face up.'

'Whose name did you use when you cast the tallies for advice, Granny?'

'My daughter-in-law's, of course.'

'That was wrong. The money is yours, so you should use your own name.'

'My own name? Ai-yo. Then I ought to go back and do it again. I hope this time it comes up positive, you know.'

The lecturer's trick worked like magic. With a slight modification in tactics, my fib had immediately lifted the dark clouds that were gathering around me. That same afternoon, the old woman returned to sign the contract; she even extended a cheerful invitation for me to visit her family. For years she'd sold dumplings from a stand in front of her house, and she hoped I'd give her a chance to thank me with free dumplings and stewed meats.

I agreed, but afterwards I always skirted round her house whenever I happened to be walking in the neighbourhood.

She earned two NT dollars for each dumpling, and I had overcharged her by a million or so. I calculated that she and her daughter-in-law would have to make more than six hundred thousand dumplings to make up the cruel difference in price. What kind of transaction was that? The divination had meant a lot to her, and she had placed her trust in me. Why would the gods have given her the sign to go ahead? For days I couldn't stop thinking about the pile of dumpling wraps beneath the overhang in front of her house. Sometimes I was startled awake by nightmarish bits of dumpling filling that littered my dreams.

That dumpling house was the last one I sold, I'll never forget it. It rained on the night I decided to leave the site. I was packing up my meagre belongings when I heard someone knocking on the glass door. I turned to see Qiuzi, who was holding a jacket over her head as rain dripped down her clean white uniform shirt.

'I wanted to surprise you,' she said.

Still feeling gloomy about the house sale, I was thrown into emotional turmoil by her sudden appearance, especially since I hadn't seen her for several days. My heart ached at the sight of her, drenched by the rain. It had obviously taken her a while to find the site. All she'd been able to remember was the temple I'd mentioned, but to my surprise she had still managed to find me. Something was wrong, however; it was only eight in the evening, the prime time for any restaurant. She should be at work.

'The door was closed, the diners couldn't get in, and my colleagues were all waiting outside.'

'What do you mean?'

'The restaurant has shut down. They were giving out discount vouchers a while ago. Obviously this was all planned.'

She was shivering, so I used the boil function on the water dispenser to make her a steaming cup of coffee. She put her wet jacket back on, but couldn't shake off the chill that was evident in her body through her sopping clothes.

'Take your clothes off. There's a dryer in this show home.'

She took a sip from the cup she held in both hands before pausing to look at me. 'How am I supposed to do that?'

'You can go inside, take off your shirt and jacket, and come out wearing your vest.'

'Are you crazy?' Cradling the cup in her hands, she looked up at the ceiling, her teeth clattering noisily.

'Or you can sit over here and I'll wrap a blanket around you.'

Her eyes misted over when she turned to look at me. I reached out to flick raindrops off the tips of her hair. After a moment's hesitation, she buried her face in my jacket and began to cry. A wind blew in with the rain, shutting a window that had been tilted open. She sat back up, took out an envelope and handed it to me.

'Take it back. I don't want to keep it.'

It was a bank deposit book. We'd agreed to put a little aside each month into a joint account.

'It's a joint account. You keep it.'

'I lost my job. From now on it'll only be your money.'

The coincidence suddenly hit me: we would be both out looking for new jobs tomorrow. 'How's this for a plan?' I said. 'We won't worry about saving money for now, since what we have here isn't even enough to buy half a toilet. Let's take a trip abroad instead. How's that? We have enough here.'

'You mean spend it all?'

'If you want,' I said as I looked into her eyes, 'we can use it for our honeymoon.'

Convinced that she had heard it wrong, she softly repeated what I had said, stopping before the last two words. She tucked her sleeve into her hand again and held her arm over her nose and quivering lips. Slightly dazed, she looked at me, her eyes tired and subdued. I wasn't sure if what I'd just said might make her cry again, for she looked like she was churning inside, yet no sound emerged.

'Or we can save it,' she said a moment later.

6

The Lai family, which had gained prominence in Central Taiwan and was commonly known as the Motor Group, dealt in fertilizer and daily necessities. They had just created a new branch, a construction division. The Motor Group had made its fortune more than two decades earlier by maintaining and repairing motors. I heard that the group's success had been based on speedy response times and incomparable post-sale service. In 1996, after predicting the money-making potential of property, the second generation of the clan was put in charge of developing the vast family holdings.

The head of the branch had studied in America. A man with a square face, he had the typical southerner's swarthy, muscular appearance that suggested efficiency and vigor. He popped two betel nuts into his mouth at a time, his cheekbones bulging as he crunched away, the veins on his nose popping red on a crimson face where his eyes burned bright.

With my résumé in his hand, he made dubious comments as he read, concerned about my frequent hops from job to job.

We hired a guy last year. Three days later he was found to have secretly copied client information all three nights . . .

Of course I wasn't talking about you. You don't look the type.

Other than that, you have a fine résumé. You were in advertising and sales, so you would survive even if the sky fell.

But you have no family. That's really sad. You should hurry up and get married.

Oh, I see you lived in Erlin, so you must be familiar with the fertilizer factory we ran back then . . .

Putting the résumé down, he tossed away one cigarette and lit another. The ashtray was crawling with cigarettes he had barely smoked, like a mound of silkworms.

I gave him a general explanation of my unmarried state: I said I had a wonderful girlfriend, but I thought I needed to accomplish something before I could have her. With a nod to show his acceptance of my reasoning, he began to rock in his soft chair, arms folded across his chest.

'I've never held a management position, but I know I could do a good job. And, Mr Chairman, I was just a little boy when we lived in Erlin, so I'm sorry to say I didn't get to see your factory. I'd like to go back for a visit one day – sometimes I feel I should get out more often.'

'No need to go there any more. The Motor Group couldn't care less about a fertilizer factory these days. You can't make much off animals.'

He spat out the chewed-up betel nuts and told to his secretary to set up a personal file for me. A pretty woman, she fluttered her eyelashes and asked him what title to use. I stood up to make room so they could talk freely. He obviously had something up his sleeve, for he looked up and said in a singsong voice:

'You'll start as a reserve supervisor and we'll see how that works out. Anyone with talent stands a good chance of promotion. I require all employees to look up into the sky daily and say whatever they want. There's only one sun here, and there's hope for anyone who learns to be loyal to it.'

His mouth fully occupied with a cigarette and betel nuts, he was saying one thing but hinting at something else. I nodded and took it all in.

On Monday three days later, I bought my very first two-piece suit. It was a slightly gaudy blue, but the azure striped tie lent me an energetic flair, as if I could walk on clouds. HR assigned me a large square desk in the last row of the sales section, against the wall, where I sat in a swivel chair facing the sales unit, with people constantly walking in and out. Off to my right, at what would be about three o'clock, I could see the boss's secretary, who crossed her legs when she talked on the phone.

That night, Qiuzi and I drank a celebratory toast to my new job and enjoyed our first meal in a French restaurant. She seemed unsure of herself, finishing her appetizer, a cold dish, very slowly. When the main course, smoked salmon, was served, she was at a total loss as to how to behave; her hands rested on the table, gripping her knife and fork tightly, as if each dish required a prayer.

'You know all these dishes. Don't forget, all we have to concern ourselves with is eating.'

'We can't be haughty.'

'No, of course not. Look, someone's eating a steak with a pet in their lap.'

'Should we really be doing this?'

'Try the escargot, Qiuzi. I didn't know they could be so tasty.'

We went window shopping at a new department store after dinner. Going from level to level on the escalators, we browsed as we strolled up and down the aisles. After cursory looks in the small appliances and mother and baby departments, we stopped at a high-end fashion counter, where the attractive garments on models accentuated Qiuzi's drab reflection in a mirror. I insisted that she try on a short coat, but she backed off after a glance at the price tag. She held her hand over her eyes, as if to block a bright light; rather than the look of pleasant surprise I'd expected, her face expressed a mix of joy and despair. She turned away, as if she'd done something wrong.

From that day on, I was up to my neck in general planning. Running like a super-charged machine, the Motor Group had three construction sites under development in one re-zoned area alone. In charge of overseeing all three projects, I combined and refined the progress reports from sales supervisors for each one; on occasion I pointed out lapses in management at a site and, using what authority I had been given, gave them a helping hand with my own opinions.

I realized that, having retreated from the front line of sales, I'd found the best vantage point from which to analyze issues and was able to offer feasible solutions objectively, while quickly pinpointing the critical likelihood of success or failure in the symbiotic relationship between advertising and sales.

My job was to synthesize the reports for my boss.

He lived on a plot of farmland behind the Seventh Re-zoned Area in the city of Taichung. Many of humanity's crises were still some way off on the horizon; the 12 September 1999 earthquake had yet to strike; SARS, the killer of the century, had not begun to cast its ghostly shadow; my dreams of the time, as well as the joys and sorrows I would later experience, were quietly fermenting away; and a relatively peaceful world continued to revolve in an orderly manner.

I would arrive at the boss's house punctually at four in the afternoon. It was an old family compound, with three cars parked at the gate. Bright red West Indian jasmine and fruit trees filled his courtyard. The season for professional baseball, his favourite sport, had begun, so I had to jump in with my briefings between innings and during commercials, stopping in mid-sentence if necessary once the fierce battle resumed. When a batter for the team he sponsored struck out or hit a home run, I would groan or cheer excitedly from where I stood behind him.

When winter brought the season to an end, I stuck to the office, awaiting instructions if his gout had flared up and he was staying at home. He would summon me to the house at around ten in the morning, by which time his toes were so swollen he couldn't walk. He lived alone in the big house with its daunting high ceiling. His moans of pain echoed in the kitchen at the back. All hell broke loose if his secretary phoned after he'd finished with his instructions to remind him of an appointment that required his attention. His personal assistant would rush in, with his driver close behind, and the two pairs of hands struggled to stuff his painful feet into large, custom-made shoes. Supported by one employee on each side, he hobbled through the garden under the grape trellis like a wounded king beating a hasty retreat from the battlefield.

By then the three cars had been moved from the gate to the side of the road awaiting action, their engines purring in the sunlight. Once the boss had finally wormed his way into the back seat of the first car, his assistant would climb in on the passenger side, from where she would give directions. The two cars behind were occupied only by the drivers. They took off like a miniature motorcade, though it still looked grand and impressive owing to the size of the cars.

I'd follow on my motor scooter, and only after they'd crossed the streets and disappeared north would I turn into a lane to head back to the office. On one occasion I was caught in a downpour, so I ducked under an overhang, from where I decided to call Qiuzi. The extension rang for a long time before she came on the line to tell me she'd just received a letter in response to a job application. I told her I'd hold the line while she opened it. I heard her open a drawer looking for a pair of scissors.

I'd have simply ripped the envelope open. If it was good news, it would still be good news even if the paper was torn, and bad news wouldn't change even if it was slit open gently from left to right. The original intention of the sender wouldn't change, while your mood could be ruined by the contents.

But I didn't push her. I wanted to tell her it was raining and that winter rain gave me an empty feeling, especially after the small motorcade had just turned a corner and disappeared from sight. *How wonderful it would be if you were sitting in one of the cars, next to me, after I had just married you and brought you out from the remote mountains of Nantou, with firecrackers snapping loudly in the groves of Mengzong bamboo along the way, and we were heading to a fancy restaurant for a happy banquet.*

She finally unearthed her scissors. Resting the headset between her chin and her shoulder, she told me to wait while she opened the envelope, going about it gently, afraid to make any noise. It really didn't matter to me, but I wouldn't try to hurry her even if she took all night. I had a sudden urge to say, *Let's get married, Qiuzi. It'll be New Year soon, and there's no rule against marrying when you're poor. We can take our time to get rich.*

At long last a reaction came from the other end. I heard a heartbreaking throaty noise, a tiny 'oh', a somewhat shameful, suppressed 'oh', a single note that she allowed to escape at the height of her disappointment. Actually, I'd already sensed it coming from the mood I was in, and I began to worry that it would characterize our life together. On the day we were married, it would likely be a tiny 'oh' also, with a small ceremony. It would be the union of two dust motes, or a loofah gourd marrying a section of Mengzong bamboo. It would be the most romantic and yet the saddest moment. It would all depend on how our hearts found the will to fight and how our love managed to rise above the mundane; if they didn't, it would end like the boss's lonely, unoccupied cars, disappearing around the corner after a fast sprint down the street.

And so I needed to cherish her at this moment. I felt like crying when I heard her 'oh', as if I myself had just been rejected. There was a great deal I wanted to say to her: *I was destined to fall in love with you, not because of your pretty face or because of the passions I feel as a man. I loved that rainy afternoon when you beckoned to me, a complete stranger with your finger, a commonplace gesture that stirred my heart, for even though you were most likely unaware of it, you treated me almost like family. Your crooked pinkie was such a tiny image, like a single feather among ten thousand angels; luckily, it wasn't blown away by the wind, but instead flew into my life.*

She was quiet after uttering that single sound. I heard her sniffling as she turned away from the headset and sensed her dimple hiding to one side; she wanted to talk to me, but her lips could only manage to quiver.

'Come out, I'll be right there.'

'I'm not crying.'

'You took too long to open the envelope.'

Quizu's phone time had ended and we were cut off. I redialled, but no one answered this time. I ran out into the rain and headed to her apartment building, where I was determined to find the courage to say all I had to say to her.

7

Towards the end of winter, the Motor Group made plans for the lunar New Year.

I wasn't sure what the scheduled activities would be; all I knew was that employees who hoped to get married had to request leave a month in advance. Qiuzi told me to hand in my request three months before the wedding, which struck the women in the personnel office as hilarious.

'Turning in the application early will convince me you're not lying,' she said.

'We can get married at the courthouse today if that's what's bothering you.'

'It not the same. You don't realize how much fun waiting can be.'

We decided on a date in the spring, after the New Year festivities, when flowers were blooming. It was her idea. In her view, year's end was the worst time to get married, because a few days later people would say we'd already been married two years. As I saw it, her being a year older would lessen the ridicule from other women.

As well as teasing me about my wedding application, people in the personnel office spread the news way too early. One day the boss called me into his office and took a bulging red envelope out from his drawer. 'I know what you need more than anything. This is just between us, so put it away.'

He followed that gesture up with a spring holiday plan: 'You won't have to spend a thing on your honeymoon, and you can cancel all your other plans. In a few days I'll announce that we've chartered a plane for an overseas trip. You and your wife will have a great time in the Maldives.'

The fat red envelope unnerved me. I was afraid that taking it would be tantamount to signing a contract to sell myself. But it was money, enough to pay for the sofa and small appliances we'd looked at. Qiuzi couldn't believe his generosity.

'You must be important to him.'

'Well, that was how I found the nerve to propose.'

'Were you proposing? It was raining that day and we were speeding along on your motor scooter.'

Too bad she was afraid of flying. The Pescadores Islands were the farthest she'd ever travelled, and that was by boat. I tried to sell her on the Maldives as a great vacation spot, though I'd never been there, and had only explored the blue skies and aquamarine seas in a travel magazine.

'The company has even hired models for a fashion show on a raised catwalk.'

That news alone excited and intrigued Qiuzi, but her enthusiasm cooled when she thought about a plane suspended in the air with no road beneath it. In the end we decided to change the location of our honeymoon. So at the same time as the company's chartered plane was taking off from Taoyuan

Airport, our hired minivan would be speeding towards Hualian, another coastal city.

The ceremony was held at Taichung District Court, followed by a celebration at a seafood restaurant for a party of five – Qiuzi's parents, her younger brother, who had just completed his military service, plus Qiuzi and me. Her father, who had a slightly bent back, whispered a question before picking up his chopsticks,

'No one else?'

I explained to him that my co-workers couldn't attend because they were on a company-sponsored tour. *But please don't worry; it's no big deal. What matters most is that I'll treat Qiuzi well and do my best to make her happy.*

When I thought about it later, I realized I'd misunderstood his comment; he was wondering why no one from my family was there.

But that didn't bother Qiuzi, since we were all family now. She got up to serve her parents and, still clad in her hired wedding dress, filled a bowl of soup for her brother. The sleeves were so long they were rolled up and bunched around the elbows, making her look like a kitchen maid who had worn a fancy dress during the day and was reluctant to take it off once night arrived.

I kept urging them to eat. As I put a prawn on the plate of each of my parents-in-law, I couldn't stop apologizing. *I'm sorry. I'm sorry; I'm really sorry.* Good thing I hadn't had anything to drink, or I'd have started blubbering. By then they'd figured out that I had no family. I didn't even own a dog, or maybe a cat, that I could have brought along, so they looked like a family of four attending my wedding, with no complaints. A few courses later, Qiuzi's mother stood up and solemnly toasted me, saying that Qiuzi had always been a sensible girl. 'If she does anything out of line, please forgive her for my sake.'

My face reddened. I wanted to say thanks, but just kept apologizing.

Qiuzi was looking calm and serene, like a true bride, despite everything.

When we returned to our flat after seeing the three of them onto the last bus home, she finally breathed a sigh of relief and laughed, still holding the bouquet. 'That was close. I told Mother not to cry; I said I wouldn't get married if she did. So she didn't. She was probably afraid I'd be a burden to them in their old age. Outrageous.'

'They won't be back up the mountain till very late, I guess.'

Yes, she said.

Then we started our life together.

That life couldn't begin without a sound. But she'd never been so quiet. She sat at the foot of the bed, her neck scrunched down between her shoulders like the wings of a butterfly frozen in a painting. I was sure she regretted laughing so soon, for once she stopped, the air congealed around us and neither of us could find our voice. We'd never spent time together in a soundless room before.

She was pinching the lacy hem of her gown, nearly tearing it off, but still not a word. I'd only held her once, in the show home on that rainy night; since then, we had stolen a few gentle roadside kisses, like pecking birds. Anything more could have happened only in my dreams. I liked her shyness, though. Over the past four years, we had not been intimate, unlike other couples who are madly in love, nor had we opened ourselves up much. Yet she always let me see what I wanted. Her eyes held a refreshing purity, an endearing transparency that revealed the true feelings and inner self of a woman in love.

I kissed the smooth, fair skin of her neck from beneath her hair down to her collar, and it was as if she'd kept her hair short for this very moment. But that wasn't quite true, because it had been short on the afternoon we first met, outside the coffee shop. Maybe she was already wearing her hair short in a previous life.

When I tried to undress her I discovered that the hired dress had ten thousand buttons running down the back. I was getting jumpy and had to use both hands. The room grew even quieter. I looked for something to say: *We have to return the dress tomorrow.*

That got a response: 'When I was a child, a firefly once flew into our house through an open window.'

'Ah, that sounds romantic. I wish we had one of those now.'

'Go and shut the window,' she murmured.

I went over, shut the window and pulled the curtain together, keeping the ceiling light on to look at her.

But she'd stepped into the bathroom, where the running water sounded hesitant at first, then weaker, and finally went off completely. Sliding the shower door partially open, she complained, 'The shower has a glass door. I didn't notice that when we rented this place.'

I hadn't either, but this gave me a chance to spy on her blurred figure. Through the watery mist, I saw that the tiled dividing wall she tried to hide behind didn't go all the way up to the ceiling; her exposed silhouette through the glass door revealed delicate curves, bent elbows, breasts, and an unfamiliar body that drifted in the steam, like a hazy dream rushing at me and turning into a naked apparition to roam amid my fears.

She was so bashful that we had to seek the cover of the blanket. It felt like a momentous family gathering around a brazier, now that New Year had just passed. We held each other around that virtual brazier and kept raising the temperature in the darkness under the blanket, where two moist bodies intertwined. I didn't show my head until I came up for air.

Finally I had a chance to ask her about the firefly. What happened after it flew in?

'I thought about a fire, of course,' she said from under the blanket.

8

Qiuzi got a job at a flower shop near our new home; she opened up early each morning for the truck which brought clusters of cut flowers from the market. I often stopped on my way to work and watched her sitting on a low stool trimming the stems. She threw the discarded leaves into a bamboo basket and laid the cut flowers on a stand to her right; the splashed water turned the ground around her muddy. From the side, the shadow she cast looked like those flowers under the morning sun.

On clear afternoons, she liked to sit on a grassy slope in the children's park, from where she could see the roof of our apartment building peeking through the treetops. She would stand and wave to me when I returned from work before bounding down the slope like a child; youngsters playing in the park would look up at her with animated gazes, as if drawn to her.

We had more to say to one another than we could fit into a night. I got used to her interruptions and usually waited to speak until she stopped to swallow, though once she had done so she would quickly continue with what she wanted to say. We were like classmates meeting at a reunion after decades, where one of them, blessed with an exceptional memory, could recall all sorts of anecdotes from their schooldays.

'Once I was running really fast, and when I neared the finish line, I heard my classmates cheering me on, something they'd never done before, strangely. So I froze. I forgot to run and started walking instead.'

'You're thin enough to be a good runner.'

'Ah, you weren't listening. I'm talking about walking to the finish line. My teacher glared at me; my classmates laughed and clapped. I got the top score only in art. In music, I just did okay, because I'd have an attack of nerves and sing off-key, changing one song into a different one.'

Why are you laughing? These are things I never told you.

When the commercial that was playing on TV ended, she'd stop talking and turn back to her favourite drama series, leaving me to go over material to submit to the boss the next day. We usually went to bed at ten o'clock, well before the time to go to sleep, because there were still many things – unimportant things – we wanted to say. Like lovebirds settling under the eaves. Her voice would be soft at such times, and she looked more feminine in a nightgown as she lay there wide-eyed, quietly concentrating on what I was saying. Her dimple would open secretly in the dim light when I talked of our dreams and aspirations.

So finally one day I told her about the goat I'd raised as a child. Black with a grey stripe around its neck, it bleated for grass every morning before I went to school. But for a while it stopped and ignored me when I offered it some grass. One morning I got up early to check on the goat and saw Father feeding it, mumbling to himself as he fed grass into the pen. When the goat was nearly full, he left the rest for me to do. Instead of going to school on the back of his bicycle that day, I ran all the way, and kept that up for several days, even vowing not to see him again, not ever.

'I regret that, Qiuzi, even now.'

'Let me try to guess what your father said to the goat.'

'Don't tell me.'

'Hmm, maybe *he* wouldn't want me to tell you either.'

We fell silent, as if affected by a sense of sorrow. She was pretending to be asleep when I got up to write a couple pages in my journal. When I heard her quietly turn over, I knew there was more she wanted to say, but was holding back. She had learned when to keep quiet, which brought me the pleasure of being understood. I secretly vowed that night never to make her sad again.

I continued to work faithfully for Boss Motor, who gradually delegated his private affairs to me – delivering money to a mistress he had stopped seeing for the time being, or sending flowers to a particular building the first minute after midnight. I also met with bank managers in the reception room by the foyer while he was watching a baseball game, chatting nonchalantly with one leg cast over the other. Sometimes, when a property broker he knew well came by, I'd ask the man to wait in the foyer so I could go inside to shout HOME RUN in front of the TV and discuss an inning that should have never, ever ended with runners on base.

When Boss Motor wanted me to go someplace with him, I rode in the second car, also a Cadillac. Finally having a passenger to talk to, the driver chattered nonstop about his pubescent, rebellious children while keeping an eye on the distance from the car ahead. As a light turned yellow and began to flash, he'd floor the pedal and shoot through the intersection so no car could cut in and stop him from following close behind the one in front.

'Sooner or later I'll go crazy, driving an empty car every day,' he said as he laid on his horn.

'How long has this been going on?'

'Since the day he lost his mind.' The driver laughed.

But it was a rare moment for me. Sitting by the window like a rich man, I gracefully parted the curtain to look at the mute ocean of humanity outside, waves of motor scooters rushing this way and that. It was hard to imagine that only a few hours earlier I'd been swimming in those very waves, wearing a fuchsia-coloured helmet whose visor kept steaming up from my sweat.

As I sat in the back seat, the pleasant smell of leather filled the Cadillac, and its profound significance was not lost on me. It had the lure of money and power, mysterious, enticing and yet out of reach. If we had some way to go to reach our destination, the image of my father, who was about the same age as my boss, would float into my mind. Such a view would have been beyond his reach if he were alive. All he could do each day was ride his bicycle to work, race home at noon to feed Mother, who had been severely disabled in a traffic accident, and then hurry back to the school before the third and last bell for afternoon classes.

Both men were members of the human race, but the difference between them couldn't have been greater.

I wished that Old Li would drive slowly into tomorrow, even well into the future, giving me time to picture myself rich enough to buy a paradise, such as this dream-like flagship sedan. Then I could wave to my parents and say, *Hop in. Finally, we're able to live like this . . .*

In addition to the free rides in his Cadillac, Boss Motor provided me with a chance to observe treacherous and fickle officialdom in action. We once went to the municipal administrative offices, where the Construction Bureau chief greeted us personally, while the head of the construction management section, a man I couldn't beg my way in to see on my own, stood with his hands stiffly at his side and offered explanations and answers to Boss Motor's enquiries. Later, when Boss Motor's gout was acting up and I went there alone, they treated me like an old friend, laying pending applications out on the table for me.

Thorny issues were resolved overnight. I returned to Boss Motor in high spirits, only to see neither a surprised nor a happy look on his face.

'Connections are bought with hard cash,' was all he said, offhandedly.

I often accompanied him to the funerals of important people. Wearing a black suit reserved for just such an occasion, together with dark glasses and a dark grey tie, he deepened the sadness around him by showing up looking like a mobster. Though he shed no tears, he wore a solemnly respectful expression and extended his sympathy in a deep, raspy voice, creating such a heartbreaking atmosphere that the bereft family would choke up with emotion as they bowed their thanks.

He was playing a role when he put himself so wholeheartedly in the shoes of a mourner. Yet under different circumstances, such as watching a ball game, he'd put all trivial matters aside and fix his gaze on a curve ball he'd wanted to see drift from the pitcher's mound, like a wind-blown willow branch ripping silently through the air. I wouldn't hear him breathe; he would regain signs of life only when the batter hung his head low, having swung and missed.

'Going out in three cars. It must be because he's lonely,' Qiuzi said.

'I don't get it either. Rich people have strange ideas.'

'Then I don't want us to be rich. I want us to be like this.'

'No. We should get rich quickly so we can understand him better.'

We were sitting up in bed, leaning against the headboard. Opposite us on the wall was a developer's poster advertising a villa; its vast garden looked like rolling green hills, with tree-lined walkways criss-crossing the development, and a meandering pond murmuring musically. When we could no longer find the words to say what we felt, we rested our sleepy eyes on the poster until a vague drowsiness crept up and took over.

It was a distant fantasy land, but we'd stared at it so often the scene began to look real.

9

We nearly failed to make it through 1999, a dark year.

A catastrophic earthquake struck late one night. Qiuzi went to pieces, even though, truthfully, it hadn't disturbed a hair on her head.

There was no prior warning. Our walls shook and then began to bulge and warp, as the glass door and windows shattered. The floor under the foot of the bed buckled, and the overhead lampshade crashed onto our blanket.

I learned later that it had originated in the depths of a distant valley, caused, so they say, by countless mad cows suddenly turning in their sleep.

I'll never forget the darkness in the room, where a strange yet familiar hum turned out to be the sound of Qiuzi trembling. I couldn't see her, but I heard her hopping up and down, unable to take an actual step. The floor was littered with glass shards that cut my feet, but I ignored the pain and finally managed to grope my way over to the corner, where she was still hopping. I grabbed her hand and we ran for our lives.

As we scurried down the winding staircase, screams

emerged from every floor, and, glancing through a window, we witnessed devastation in the lane outside, where distant searchlights cast a flickering red glow. I kept dragging Qiuzi with me, unaware that something had gone wrong with her, even when we finally made it out of the apartment building. She could still speak then. 'Where are we?' she asked in a shaky voice.

'Don't worry. The park is up ahead.'

The unlit park was shrouded in shadows and submerged in a cacophony of noise from the shouting of names and the incessant crying of children. Within moments, powerful aftershocks struck, sending heavy objects crashing down from places too high to be visible, as wailing fire engines sped down the streets.

For a while I lost Qiuzi, who had been pushed to the edge of the park by the fleeing crowds. It took me a while to locate her on the slope where she had often waved to me. With her arms around her knees, she was shaking uncontrollably. We'd not had time to grab a blanket on our way out, and had certainly never anticipated such a terrifying moment. Her hands were icy cold, as were the soles of her feet, for she'd lost her slippers in the mayhem.

Over the next few hours the crowd slowly dispersed, some residents returning to their buildings with lingering fear, some squeezing into their parked cars to keep warm, while others left in vehicles that drove off in a stream. The sky was beginning to lighten, but Qiuzi shook her head, refusing to go back inside. Her eyes glazed over as she stared at the trees skimming the rooftops across the way.

I wouldn't have been preoccupied with making phone calls if I'd known that something had gone wrong with her.

I couldn't reach Boss Motor and had no news from the company. When the sun peeked through the clouds, I left the park to buy something to eat and told Qiuzi to stay where she was.

My colleagues had trickled in to the office by the time I arrived. One woman's house had completely collapsed. Boss Motor was giving orders, assigning each of us to a neighbourhood. We were told to return to the office immediately after conducting an on-site inspection and to refrain from offering personal opinions to the residents. If we saw any severe damage, we were to rush back and tell him.

I was assigned to a building with over three hundred mixed-use units. The ground floor was fronted with thriving shops, while about a thousand people called the upper floors home. When I reached it, I stopped and sought the shade of a row of ancient trees, afraid to look at the spot where the tall building stood. Apparently I was still plagued by the spectre of death, even after all these years. Now the answer hung in the air in front of me, and I had only to look up to see if the structure had withstood the quake. Instead I squinted as if going blind.

And so the moment my hesitant gaze finally fell on the building, still standing tall under the sun, I wept like a fool. I raced back to the office with the good news. Then the general manager gave the latest count: at least two thousand had died, many more were missing or injured, and more than ten thousand houses had collapsed. Other damage statistics were still being tallied.

At first Boss Motor was speechless after hearing the reports, but then a rapturous look appeared on his face, as if he'd been struck by an epiphany. He surmised that banks would freeze construction funds in the wake of the disaster, forcing

many companies to shut down. He rattled off a list of potential losers, including a few of our fiercest competitors and his
most hated enemies. He told us to shout a slogan with him,
followed by loud clapping:

'We are – still standing.' He ended the rally with one last
repetition of it, shouted on a high note.

But Qiuzi was not standing.

She was nowhere in sight when I rushed back to the
children's park for her, only to find the soymilk and sesame
flatbreads I'd bought for her lying untouched on the grass. Is
she family? a woman asked, when she saw me running around.
They took her to the hospital.

The doctors told me that during my two-hour absence she
had passed out from hypothermia, but that there was no
obvious sign of any other illness. I took her straight home,
though it no longer looked like home when I opened the door.
Everything was strewn across the floor, but the walls had not
collapsed. The poster we'd stared at every night had peeled off
the wall and was swaying limply in the autumn wind coming
through the broken window.

Qiuzi quit her job at the florist's. She sat in the sun on the
balcony in the mornings, but mysterious dizzy spells would
grip her in the afternoons, making it impossible for her to go to
the park to wait for me after work. But that wasn't the worst of
it. She began to show troubling symptoms after nightfall, when
she could be racked with alternating chills and fever, or throw
up the little bit of food she had managed to get down at dinner.

After her second check-up, Qiuzi was said to have some
syndrome or other, an accumulation of protracted fear and
loneliness, which had flared up in the aftermath of the disaster.
The doctor could offer no medication, and said she'd get over it

in time with help from her family. What an unhelpful prognosis – and from a physician, no less. Getting over it wasn't going to be easy. There is nothing worse than being stuck at some point in life, unable to move forward or backward. I didn't know what had got her stuck, and only stammered a response when the doctor asked me what she feared and loved the most. She was so adorable that I'd fallen in love with her before I knew it, or knew much about her, and I'd never had a chance to probe her inner world.

I could only think back to the dark night of the quake and why she'd kept hopping around. We'd been no more than five or six feet apart, and I could have wrapped my arms around her if I'd taken only a couple of steps towards her, but the darkness at that moment had placed us in two separate worlds.

But I wanted to help her. I cleaned the flat, repaired the cracks in the wall myself, and searched for new furnishings to brighten up the bleak surroundings. Then I spent our last savings on hardwood flooring so that she could sit or lie down any time she wanted.

She loved to lie on the floor; drawn by the rich but subtle smell of wood, she'd stay there a long time. A hint of happiness slowly took over her sluggish body and mind, and she finally felt like talking again. Still unable to recall much herself, she wanted me to tell her some amusing anecdotes from my life.

Sure, I could tell her stories, but not amusing anecdotes. I racked my brain but realized how boring a life I'd lived, having travelled through a barren field of existence. I tried to go back to early childhood, taking pains to avoid sad stories that would upset her, but just about everything in my past was woeful.

'Then tell me something you've done that's embarrassing.'

'For a while I thought my father was a primary school principal.'

'Oh. Wasn't he?'

'Wait, I've got something!'

I'd finally hit upon a mildly sad story that might sound amusing: when I was seven years old, the proudest year of my life, we lived for free in a hut with a thatched roof, a loan from the village chief, who had used it to store fertilizer and a water pump. In it I cooked sweet sticky rice balls for the winter solstice over briquettes. Some were as red as peach flowers, others as white as plum blossoms. When they had all floated to the surface I went to pick up the pot, but knocked it over and spilled them all over the floor. Even so, they tasted great. Father ate three bowlfuls when he returned from work. I was slower, because I had to bite each one in half in order for my mother to enjoy them.

'Why did you have to bite them in half?' Qiuzi asked.

'Um, she had a small mouth.'

Finally I'd made her laugh, though she was cautious and pressed her hand against her chest to stifle her laughter.

Qiuzi began to recover slowly once October had passed. The bad dreams, however, continued almost nightly, and she would jam her feet into her slippers the very second she woke up. The 1.47 a.m. earthquake had stamped its image on her mind, and I assumed she was just easily frightened. But then one day she said, 'Our house caught fire when I was a child. It burned until the crossbeam fell. I had an older sister, but she was charred into a black lump.'

I suddenly recalled her reference on our wedding night to fireflies. At the time, it seemed to have come out of nowhere, and for me she had just been a charming, bashful bride. Now I saw it was a heartbreakingly sad association with traceable origins, like the scar on the side of her breast, which she pointedly hid at night. No wonder she was fearful when our window was left open, and no wonder even a firefly would worry her.

What was wrong with us? Had we become a couple only because we were connected by similar fates?

One night she sobbed as she related a dream she'd had about her parents being pinned under a bed by a collapsed wall. The village chief sent two backhoes to dig them out, but they came down too hard and chopped off one leg, two legs . . . It began to rain, the first rain of that autumn, as she recalled that dream. She craned her neck and listened intently, the sound of the rain seeming to restore her sense of clarity. Then she simply bounded into another scene from the story and continued talking as if still in her dream. 'I was too scared to sleep any time I heard rain dripping in through our leaky roof. But you know, ever since I left home I've really missed the rain. The whole family was home on rainy days.'

'That's right, like us at this moment.'

'No, it's not the same. You've never heard rain like that. The wind blew when it rained, making a rustling noise in the bamboo grove, like stirring beans in a pan. It wasn't loud, but I heard it.'

'When I get some time off, we're going to bring those sounds back with us.'

There was a long pause before she said, sounding disappointed, 'I know you're very busy.'

She was right. No one at the company had had any time off for two months in a row. The bleak housing market was chillier than a world of ice and snow. Clients who had signed contracts just before the quake demanded refunds, while those who had placed advance orders two years before refused to take up their ownership. Boss Motor had to ask for funds from the parent company, resulting in a personal visit from his father one morning. Leaning on a cane and bent with fury, the moment he walked in, the eighty-five-year-old man gave his son a humiliating tongue-lashing.

Desperate for a solution, Boss Motor told me to help the old man out of the office. 'Tell him we've already come up with an emergency plan for next month. Now I'm expecting a client any minute.'

'Totally incompetent. I'm cancelling the baseball team sponsorship, and don't ever come to me for money again.'

The office was deathly quiet. I accompanied the old man and his cane into the lift and went with him up to the rooftop garden.

I couldn't make the trip I'd promised Qiuzi. She would be fast asleep when I got home each night, a simple dinner laid out on the table untouched. A tiny light would be on, and the flat would feel as cold as the housing market.

Sometimes I sat on the edge of the bed to gaze at her face. She looked bony and gaunt after what she'd been through. I wanted to wake her up, but was afraid to interrupt her sleep, her self-induced therapy, so I just waited by her side. I didn't do what I should have done. If, during that terrifying moment on the night of the earthquake, I had remained calm and cool but decisive, I would have wrapped a blanket around her and hidden with her under the bed, instead of dragging her out and running without thinking. As it was, she must have lost her inner self along the way, leaving behind only a dazed body by the time we reached the park. The building had survived the earthquake, so fleeing heedlessly had not been the right thing to do. I had been running all these years, ever since primary school, and it turned out that this time I was wrong to run. She was merely an innocent bystander, an unlucky girl I'd dragged along behind me.

Generally ignorant of what the future holds, when something happens, we call it fate. But at that moment, I struggled, as if wrestling with fate, unwilling to accept that my future could be so pallid. Quietly putting the cold food into my mouth, I couldn't stop tears from falling into my bowl. At least a sense of tenderness lingers when two people face hardships together; eating alone, on the other hand, means being confronted by solitary misery. As I ate I waited, like a refugee who has escaped starvation only to find himself adrift in a dark sea, for Qiuzi to open her eyes.

Certainly, in hindsight, I should have been pleased with how things were back then. Yes, she was ill, but at least she was still with me, and I could hold her hand as I waited for her to wake up.

Later I was struck by the strange thought that maybe there was a certain sound of rain that could save her. After visiting several music stores, I finally got a response of sorts from one, a shop that had a practice room, where a woman sat at the piano. I stood behind her until she finished a piece, and then asked her about an instrument used to accompany singing, trying to make myself understood with hand gestures as I told her it was shaped like a bone, something you hold in your hand and shake to make a rustling, mournful sound.

'What do you want it for?'

'Rain—'

'You want to shake it when it rains?'

'No. It sounds like rain when you shake it.'

She nodded with a puzzled look. 'It sounds like a sand-bell to me.'

'Is there sand inside? If so, that must be it.'

'But it doesn't sound like rain to me. It doesn't have the feel of rain.'

Wanting to be helpful, she flipped through a booklet and made three phone calls, but failed to produce a better answer, so she asked, 'Have you ever seen one?'

I shook my head. 'I only know it makes a rustling sound.'

An expression of 'what exactly do you want' appeared on her face, but at least she didn't give up. Someone like her would surely be reborn as a kindly person in her next life. Knitting her brow, she looked thoughtfully at a poster on the wall and then blurted out, 'Hold on, I've got an idea. I think I saw something like that at a concert with bamboo instruments.'

She made another phone call, this one lasting until she was hoarse.

She wrote down an address for a workshop that specialized in bamboo instruments. They developed them for themselves, so they might be reluctant to sell me one.

'But you can give it a try, now that you know what you're looking for,' she said.

She was right about that. I'd get them to sell me one if I had to get down on my knees and beg. As I was walking out, she sat down at the piano, raised the lid, turned and added, *It's called a rainstick, or a rain club. That's something I just learned.*

I found the workshop at the address she'd given me. It was quite late by the time I left with the rain club I'd worked hard to obtain. On my way home, I couldn't resist the temptation to take it out and study it. It was as long as a bamboo piggy bank

I'd had as a child and looked like a sword if you carried it across your body. But it was a comforting sword. The baby-faced bamboo artisan had given me a demonstration by tilting it to one side and then the other, controlling the rainfall sound by shaking it faster or slower.

'You can treat it like an hourglass.'

'You're right. It makes a sandy sound.'

'Your wife is a very lucky woman,' she said.

Downstairs in our apartment building, in the dim, deserted stairwell, I took it out and gave it one more practice shake at the night sky . . .

Quietly changing into my pyjamas once I was inside our flat, I tiptoed up to the bed, where Qiuzi was fast asleep, feeling as if I'd returned from deep in the mountains with a secret antidote. Knowing that this was the best I could do, I felt like crying and yet was filled with anticipation. I tilted the rain club to one end, shook it gently, and gingerly tilted it back to the other end, sending the sound of falling rain up to her ears, as I'd intended.

A rustling sound of stirred beans in a bamboo grove spread through the room.

Her eyes opened slightly, like stars beginning to lighten up a dark night. Taking hold of my sleeve, she pulled me towards her and then pushed me away, like a swing. The 'rain' grew louder from the force of shaking – the sound of falling rain as gusting wind swept through the bamboo grove.

'How did you think of that? Why are you so good to me?'

It was just a long section of a bamboo. What was in it? A bunch of fine sand, I assumed. It created a fleeting illusion, but now she was fully awake, a bright light was shining in her eyes; she sat up and leaned against me, tears rolling down her cheeks.

We each gave it another shake. She shook it so hard it sounded like the beans were being turned over in the grove.

Then she threw herself on me. Her body had grown slack over time, and it felt as if she completely covered me, chest to chest, pores against pores. She talked haltingly, and I could feel her breath through her lips, sweet, with warm saliva, as if some intimate part of her had opened a hot spring for me.

It felt as if it were raining in the room.

The rustling sound continued – *sha sha* . . .

10

Apparently alarmed by the depressed post-earthquake housing market, Boss Motor forced himself to come to work every day, sometimes wearing oversized slippers that exposed a purple sheen stretching from his red, swollen toes to his ankles. Since the scolding from his old man, he had greeted every visiting bank manager, showing restraint in his interactions and never forgetting to present them with parting gifts and bid them farewell with excessive, open-eyed deference until the lift doors closed. He came alive as soon as the guests were gone, telling me to phone anyone who could tell him the latest baseball score. *Is the game over? Did Leftie come to their rescue?*

Some six months into the housing market recession, we began to hear of lay-offs at construction companies. Builders whose structures had collapsed fled to the West Coast of the USA or to Canada. Those who still had unsold units were plagued by an absence of buyers, and even price reductions couldn't bring them back. A fear of high-rises continued to spread, and any attempt at marketing them or putting them in fancy packaging simply amounted to throwing good money away.

One day Boss Motor called me into a secret room.

'This may not seem like much, but it's off-limits to most people.'

Windowless, the room was about thirty square metres in size, the ventilator roaring like a swarm of mosquitoes.

He recited the names of people who had made secret visits there, some of whom were from the Legislative Yuan, while others were favoured nominees for the Control Yuan, all of them officials in high positions.

'Cigars are symbols of power. I think it's time for you to have a taste.'

In the secret room were two drinks cabinets, next to which stood a glass box that looked like the kind of ice chest you'd find in a school tuck shop.

'Here are the world's finest cigars,' he said as he opened the glass lid. 'Pick one.'

I'd never even smelled a cigar. I could only swallow and wonder why I was getting this special treatment.

'Cuban cigars are the most expensive. Try this one.'

He took out a semi-circular cigar cutter to snip the ends off and, with a flick of his pistol lighter, the two cigars were soon burning bright red as if they were the last flames of the century. During the market slide his brothers had ridiculed him mercilessly. After handing me one of the cigars, he opened his mouth wide and launched a fierce assault on the Cuban cannon, which began to spew angry smoke.

'At times like this, you win if you stay put and do nothing,' he said.

'I came up with an idea for a joint sales centre to dispose

of all the unsold units,' I said. 'I've been talking to people about using the empty plot by the farmer's market for a makeshift sales promotion centre. When it's ready, we can push all the projects.'

'That's a damned good idea. I knew you'd been thinking.'

'Is there anything else you'd like me to do, Mr Chairman?'

'Hold on, young man, I'm about to get you drunk.'

He talked with his mouth full, the brown cannon slurring his words as if he was murmuring private thoughts. He had to take a quick puff in mid-sentence to keep the flame of war on the tip burning bright. I realized that his hands were occupied in uncorking a bottle of red wine held between his knees. The corkscrew must have gone in cockeyed, for it came out with broken bits of cork that rained down on the crotch of his trousers.

I was no help. I'd never smoked a cigar *and* I'd never tasted red wine. I could only stupidly watch what he was doing and listen carefully for whatever words might emerge out of the corner of his mouth. *Join me in a glass. Fuck.* That last word came through clear as a bell.

'I thought I'd be safe not surfing during the tsunami, but it turns out that sunbathing on the beach is even more danger-ous. How about this? Now that you've come up with the idea of joint sales, I'll add a special bonus with each purchase. For anyone who signs a contract now, the company will pay the mortgage interest for the first two years. How do you think that will work? What we need to do now is recover our capital as quickly as possible. If it drags on like this, it'll kill me.'

'It'll definitely work. But are you sure you want to do that, Mr Chairman?'

'You think my old man will be against it, don't you? But,

you know, if we can't move these units, he'll suffer too.'

He filled his glass and emptied it in three gulps. As he poured himself another, he urged me to drink up. I picked up the long-stemmed glass and took a sip. Something rich and intoxicating rushed to my head via the tip of my tongue and my palate. The wine had a hint of sunshine that immediately blunted the lingering taste of the cigar.

Now I'd savoured two luxuries, but there had to be something hidden beyond the spiciness and redolence, something I didn't understand. That was especially true of the cigar; though I couldn't say exactly what it symbolized, just holding it in my hand gave me a sense of power more formidable than even that gained from wielding a samurai sword.

'You look like someone born to smoke cigars and drink red wine. You'll be hooked one of these days. I believe I've read you correctly. You had such a determined gaze in your eyes when you came for the interview, you looked like you were volunteering for a suicide mission. You must have had a tough life and more than your share of hardships. But that's all right. The end may be in sight.'

'I'm doing okay now.'

'Wouldn't you like to do even better?'

I didn't know what to say. Though his question caught me by surprise, the intoxicating prospect he held out made my heart race.

'I'd already been to America and cycled through five colleges by the time I was your age. I married the prettiest campus queen on the East Coast. You probably aren't aware that my father has three wives. My mother is number three. I wouldn't have come back if it hadn't been for the fight over our inheritance.'

He paused and took such a long drag on his Cuban cigar that its tip burned as bright as his bloodshot eyes. 'Just look at what's happening out there, at the state we're in after two thousand years. If we keep going like this, the brothers will really have something to laugh about. Wife number one hired the general manager, and the CFO is related to wife number two. Get the picture? Every one of the people around you is up to no good.

'I want you to be my trusted aide and leave the company with me,' he said quietly, blowing out smoke.

My cigar had gone out earlier, so I relit it with his lighter and copied him by taking a deep drag through quivering lips. I sensed something I hadn't expected in the aroma, a penetrating fragrance that seemed to travel deep into my heart.

I waited for details, which I expected to be fantastic, such as where he wanted to take me, and how it would be a better place than this. Naturally, I wanted something for both Qiuzi and me.

'Now I'll tell you something. I'm keeping the GM here to deal with the aftermath, while you and I go to Taipei. We've received permission to develop a large hillside plot. Since the earthquake has made villas the preferred dwelling type, we have to seize this heaven-sent opportunity. This is the largest piece of all our ancestral land, so everyone's salivating over it. You'll stay close to me and help me fend off the schemers. Besides which, this will be a chance to show off your talent. I guarantee you'll enjoy an early retirement with more than you can spend in a lifetime.'

Never much of a drinker, I was a little tipsy when I stood up, after only a few sips.

While I was turning to leave that secret room, Boss Motor stopped me with a question:

'Do you know why I picked you?'

I was clueless. The words unfurled through a mouthful of cigar smoke.

Sincerity.

11

Qiuzi went back to work at the florist's.

A doleful expression had crept onto her face since her illness, and the tips of her hair, which had grown longer, swayed, giving her the air of a woman who had been through a great deal. I'd wanted to suggest that she get a haircut, but thought better of it. The illness had given me a more mature Qiuzi. I liked the change. Maybe the longer hair would add allure to her face, and it wouldn't be simply because she was adorable that I loved her. I wanted to love her for all she was.

I wolf-whistled under my breath when I walked past the florist. As I watched her pick out flowers with a customer or help lovers pair roses or lilies with baby's breath, the sight of her thin figure pained me. It had me thinking that if one day I could take on her illness, I probably wouldn't feel as bad as I did at that moment.

One rare night she said she wanted to go out, so after dinner I suggested we go to the cinema. She changed her mind halfway there. 'Window shopping doesn't cost anything. We haven't done that in a long time.'

That was fine with me; I didn't care where we went. Watching a film was important to me, but it was nothing compared with making her happy. So we'd window-shop. If we saw something we liked we could buy it; people should never window-shop just because it's free. Are there people who walk the halls of a hospital to avoid being sick?

But I didn't say any of this to her. The department store was having an anniversary sale, and each counter had a discount sign to thank its customers. We took the lift to the top floor, where we switched to an escalator to descend one floor at a time. I'd kicked myself for not insisting on buying her the coat that earlier time, so this time I stealthily picked up two silk scarves and tucked them under my arm. I also had my eye on a turtleneck sweater; if she liked it, I'd spend whatever it cost to keep her well.

She found me out when I stood in the queue to pay, and put them all back.

'If you must buy something, we need a kettle.'

So in the small appliance department she picked out an apple green enamel kettle barely big enough to feed a bird. The narrow spout looked like a pouting mouth.

'It's too small. Look at the mouth. Like it's asking for more water.'

'You're so good to me that I'll add water just for you.'

I had to hide my feelings. Her frugality was a reflection of my deficiencies. I had trouble understanding how a woman could endure this kind of material deprivation. She'd once had a fuchsia lipstick, which she refused to replace once it was used up. Without its lustre, her lips were so pale it was as though she'd gone for three days without food.

The week before, she'd been angry at herself for getting ill, saying she needed to get better so that she wouldn't drag me down.

The next day she went out to skip rope in the park. Through the window I saw petite shoulders bouncing up and down, a solitary, lonely sight as the fading late-afternoon light shone down on each turn of the rope, like the illusion of happiness now lost.

Now that we'd bought the kettle, she wanted to go home before we'd visited even half the store.

I returned with the thoughts I'd left with still stuck in my throat. I'd planned to tell her everything on the way out and surprise her with the happy news about my chance for a better life for us. But then it occurred to me that she hadn't yet completely recovered, and my imminent departure for the north might be too much for her. What was most exasperating was my sudden confusion: not going to Taipei would be fine if it were just for myself, but this was for her, and yet I couldn't bring myself to tell her about it.

Maybe my problem was in overthinking; Qiuzi, on the other hand, couldn't keep anything inside her. She talked fast, eager to say what was on her mind. Once the things that made her happy began to dwindle, she had nothing more to add, and for days simply repeated herself.

Would she have turned those stale topics over and over like that if she'd been happy?

I was still considering the best way to tell her when the moment passed.

And I had underestimated the kettle. As I said, we are forever ignorant of what the future holds for us. I never expected that a tiny kettle would upend the tidiness of our life together. The mouth-like spout had in fact brought with it bad luck, and by the time the first plume of watery steam rose from its spout, it had already blemished my life in mysterious ways.

III

Who else would you have seen if you hadn't met us?

Something trivial was likely what started it all, Miss Baixiu, and if that was what changed our love, then it was the sort of love only petty people care about. Yet, everything underwent a dramatic change simply because Qiuzi bought a kettle.

We made tea that night after happily returning home with our little kettle. Drinking tea under the pouty gaze of the tiny apple-green spout, we had no idea that, besides emitting steam, it had also secretly turned on a switch in our life. You can call it fate, Miss Baixiu, which is how many people define unfathomable, crucial changes. But for me it was perfectly clear that it was all because of that kettle.

So now I must tell you that the raffle ticket that came with the purchase of the kettle won us a single lens reflex camera.

I had no premonition of what awaited us on the day the draw for the raffle was held. It was just another Sunday. Qiuzi wanted to do something to mark the high regard in which Boss Motor held me, so we had a nice lunch at a diner that specialized in local cuisine.

'This feels strange. Are we really celebrating, when you're about to leave me?'

In truth, I hadn't shared my concerns with her. She thought about the earthquake every once in a while, and sometimes the slightest noise would give rise to unrealistic fears. To make matters worse, when I left, she would have to take care of everything, from morning to night, by herself. Although there were no signs of worry on her face, when she spoke, the happy lilt in her voice had disappeared.

As we walked past the department store after lunch, a cheering crowd had gathered in the small square in front of the entrance, even spilling out onto the flowerbeds under the roadside trees. At that moment, a moment devoid of any significance, a loudspeaker squawking out the winning raffle numbers announced Qiuzi's name. She clutched my hand in disbelief and, after hearing her name repeated, squeezed her way up through the crowd. As if it knew that the winner had been located, the loudspeaker fervidly shouted out the top prize.

Qiuzi turned to look at me before jumping up and down in the middle of all those people.

How bizarre, Miss Baixiu, that such a tragedy could be born out of joy. We bought a kettle that got us a camera, which unexpectedly set us on a course to the Luo family house six months later.

1

Taipei County's Xindian River coursed swiftly through canyons amid the hills under a clear early-spring sky.

The ancestral property acquired by the Motor clan twenty years earlier looked out over three valleys, each with a different vista; water to the east rippled southward down to a lowland below cliffs, where it turned to reveal a broad view of the teeming city of Taipei. Once permission to develop was granted, a unique layout finally emerged for the property: a school, a market, a car park, a flood prevention pond, a children's park and a community centre, as well as a hot springs site and a street lined with retail shops, the latter two still in the planning stage.

Temporary roads for construction equipment reached all corners of the site, with six yellow diggers scattered amid gentle slopes and on high ridges. Day in and day out, the only movements were those of digging and filling. Sand rose into the air whenever one of the diggers excavated a jagged boulder, which was carried off to the horizon amid the rumble of machines.

A makeshift clubhouse was built on a scenic outcrop with a fantastic view. The construction headquarters were located on the ground floor, while the second level was split into offices and a briefing room. On the day the second generation of the Motor clan arrived with their families, I saw figures moving through the upstairs windows. The noisy children had a grand time, laughing and shouting as they chased each other around a covered terrace.

Wearing a summer hat, I shuttled back and forth across a slope that was still under construction and draped in netting. The spring shrubbery was a lush green, clusters of Taiwanese hibiscus and Korean sweetheart trees all but filled the ridges, and azaleas bloomed in reds and whites by the roadside ditch. In the distance the transplanting of mature Taiwanese beech trees was under way; a crane slowly rose up, its cable quaking slightly in the air, causing the old trees to shed their denuded limbs.

When the roar of machinery stopped from time to time, I heard shouts and the banging of desks through an upstairs window. The frolicking children were called back inside as one of the adults shut the windows, muffling angry voices that now sounded like people talking with hands clamped over their mouths to stifle their rage. When the crane was back in motion they were drowned out again, as diggers started clawing up soil on another hill.

There were eight sons in the second generation of the Motor clan. Two practised medicine and one was in tech; the others ran traditional enterprises passed down from their father. The youngest son, my boss, caused the others to lose sleep. They worried about his authority over the group's construction branch, most likely because his mother was the third wife, of a lowborn lineage. He was inevitably queried about every aspect of the large-scale development project.

In questioning the eighth son's leadership ability, one faction advocated selling the whole lot, all thirty acres of it.

Another faction was reluctant to turn over family property to outsiders, and suggested looking for a prominent public construction firm to co-develop the lot.

Boss Motor left the family meeting looking grim. Tall and swarthy, he appeared older than his years and looked to be the brother who had suffered the most setbacks. He walked up a steep slope and pissed into the valley below, waiting for his brothers to leave in their cars before lighting a cigarette and taking a long drag to smoke out his unhappiness.

He asked if I was ready. I said I was. I'd changed out of my sneakers into leather dress shoes.

His driver pulled up in an SUV. We climbed into the back, where I took a canvas bag out from under the seat and opened it for him to take another look. Its eye-popping contents, every last banknote, still lay quietly inside. Boss Motor had probably done this so often it didn't even register with him, but it was my first time. I liked money perfectly well, but so much of it all in one place made me nervous. Money is a pass that can open all doors, but at this moment it felt to me like contraband that must be hidden.

We arrived at a teahouse in downtown Xindian ahead of the other party. Boss Motor and I sat at separate tables, even ordered different drinks. I was in charge of the canvas bag, which I anchored between my feet. Taking small sips of hot ginger tea, I focused my attention on movements beyond the window. He would signal to me with his eyes once they reached an agreement, and I would follow the other party outside to put the bag in the boot of his car.

During the prolonged wait for the other party, Boss Motor stared at the empty doorway. He couldn't keep quiet. With his broad, solid back to me, he said, like one spy to another: 'They wanted to sell the land and put the money in their pockets to feel safe, the motherfuckers. Do they have any idea that I take risks like this every day?'

Unaccustomed to talking to someone's back, I took another sip without responding.

'Now you see why I wanted you to come to Taipei with me, don't you?'

'Sin-cerity,' I replied before I swallowed the tea.

A quarter of an hour later the man finally showed up. Trying not to look at his face, I saw only that he was wearing a windcheater as he slipped in like a shadow. Sincerity. So as not to hear a shred of their whispered conversation, I made an effort to focus on the song playing in the teahouse, one by the famous Taiwanese singer Jody Jiang. When the song ended, I turned my thoughts to Qiuzi and what she looked like when she sunned herself in the park, or when she was on the phone asking everyone she knew how to use our windfall, the camera.

I managed to carry out my mission that day. I had only been aware of problems with water conservation on the slope, of minor flaws in the retaining wall on the shady side of the hill, of the continuing evaluation of our environmental impact, and of a delay in the granting of permits for odds and ends. I didn't want to know about anything else, not the intended recipient of the money, nor what barrier could be broken with it. I hoped I hadn't come to Taipei just to do this.

Boss Motor looked to be in seventh heaven, obviously satisfied with what he'd heard from the other man. He made two phone calls and had the SUV take us to a small hotel, where he sent the driver away and took me up in the lift. The descending dusk showed through the window of a small reception room off the upstairs hallway. The room was empty. A pair of lamps on tea tables blurred the line between day and night.

'Relax. I'll call a few out for you to choose from.'

I was still puzzling over his comment when a middle-aged woman walked up, followed by a long line of legs with white knees that led up to something surreal, like a dream. I looked down at the red carpet and stared dumbly at a bunch of red and white shoes.

The woman chatted with Boss Motor in such a familiar way they might as well have been next-door neighbours. Suddenly she whispered something to him before shoving him away by the shoulder with a yelp. He stood up, walked over, put his arm around one of the willowy waists, and headed towards the lift.

'They're all very nice,' he turned to say. 'You came on the right day.'

I fled downstairs to the lobby to wait for him. My heart was beating wildly, either because the girls were all too beautiful or because it was my first visit, and my eagerness to adjust had surpassed my feelings of alarm. Then again, it could also have been because I thought I'd never do anything like that, and felt somewhat – somewhat reluctant to pass up the opportunity. I didn't quite understand where that desire came from, but it was exciting enough for me.

I was surprised to see the willowy waist and perky derrière step out of the lift as I savoured the dream-like sensation. After briefly hesitating at the front door, she changed direction,

headed over to the sofa, and sat down beside me, then took
something out of a bag and stuffed it into her mouth. Keeping
an eye on the lift, I was wondering why she'd decided to sit by
me when she handed me the bag.

'Beef jerky. I know you're waiting for him. Why don't you
try some, to kill time?'

'Why didn't he come down with you?'

'I can't bad-mouth a guest.'

'So – do you have to wait for him too?'

'Why should I? It was over in no time, so now I have to
wait for the car to come and pick me up.'

The beef jerky was so spicy there were tears in my eyes. I
stopped chewing and just held it in my mouth.

2

Qiuzi was in the habit of placing her nightgown within reach at the head of the bed so she could easily pick up a corner to cover her chest; she didn't mind exposing her naked body, but was reluctant to show me the scar on her left breast. That modest habit showed how a woman will insist on preserving a pristine body even after she marries. In fact, the scar wasn't very big, no more than half the size of a palm print. But the skin was wrinkled, unlike a normal birthmark, which is smooth.

It really was just a wrinkle on her heart. Every time I saw her cover it, I wondered whether she was being foolish or whether she just loved me too much. And so I wanted to hold her tight, scar and all, until she murmured as she tried to catch her breath. To me her body was not simply a part of her as a woman – it was almost like my second self. There ought not to be a distinction between the two, nor any hidden space between them.

She probably didn't understand how I felt. Or maybe she did, but couldn't come to terms with an imperfect self, so she made love only with what she considered the attractive part of her body.

Treating my first night back from Taipei as our second wedding night, she remained true to form, shyly keeping her nightgown close by the whole time, so that in the dim lamplight an old and insignificant blemish took on the appearance of a lonely eye she kept blinkered.

But I still caught an occasional fleeting glimpse of it. No matter how hard she tried to cover it, that eye broke free of her nightgown each time she turned or rolled over; the lonely eye, replete with sorrow accumulated over the years, opened to me. I respected her wishes, and yet couldn't resist taking a peek, which regrettably divided my attention during our lovemaking. Half of me continued with her, while the other half longed to see it again and again, like making love to two Qiuzis, one watching me secretly, the other holding me tightly.

Her eyes glazed over in a misty white as she appeared to shudder. No matter how shy she was, there was a moment when her body separated itself from her mind, and she could no longer hide anything. Under that thin veneer lay a land turned fertile after a long drought. On a spring night that was long in coming, she tried to climb on top, but I overwhelmed her with strength I hadn't known I possessed.

It was the middle of the night, but still we got up to make tea, and she recounted her troubling days of the past week. She left for her morning job at the florist's, but had to find other ways to keep busy in the afternoon all the way up to sunset. Then, during the long night that followed, she did nothing but stare at the TV, pretending I was beside her, eventually dozing off in the chair until she awoke hours later and went into the bedroom to wait for the morning to arrive.

'What about you? You must have had a good time up in the mountains.'

'I was reminded of what you said about Mengzong bamboo when I saw a grove of it. So I carefully pushed the leaves aside to study the cracks in the topsoil. You said something about bamboo shoots breathing in the ground, but all I heard was my own breath.'

'You idiot. Mengzong bamboo is a speciality of my home-town.'

'I saw tips poking through the soil, but I wasn't sure if they were bamboo or their shoots.'

She held her arm in front of her face and laughed. She wanted to know what else, besides coming across bamboo, had happened to me up in the mountains.

How could I tell her all about the whole mountain when just talking about bamboo made her laugh? I skipped all the trivia related to the slope development and focused on the lively, vibrant landscaping and tree planting. In ten years, the maple trees would grow into a grove, the azaleas would bloom year round in every corner, and the bishop wood trees would soon form a canopy over the paths, blotting out the sweltering sun's rays when you walked under them even in the height of summer.

'I slept in the temporary clubhouse and heard them arguing over money a few days ago.'

'So they have worries too.'

'It's not so bad for them, actually. It's worse when you're poor and you argue.'

'Mmm. And so, did he win the argument?'

And then, and then I said that Boss Motor had played baseball in a big league, so he wouldn't admit defeat even if his team was losing seven to one. I couldn't tell her what happened after that and after that – that a woman sat down beside me at sundown and offered me beef jerky.

'My turn,' she said.

'You can talk till daybreak. I'll sleep on the train back to Taipei.'

And then Qiuzi embarked on a beginner's journey with her camera. She'd sought advice from some camera buffs, and had bought a book on photography. One of her friends recommended taking a class to speed up the learning process. She'd had her first class the day before.

'It's free. Once a week.'

She brought out her camera, cradling it as if it were a baby, even talking to it.

'Have you already taken some shots?'

'Not yet. I don't dare. I know the first one will be hideous. But I raised my hand in class and asked what a beginner like me should take pictures of first, people or landscapes. Everyone was looking at me. Outrageous.'

'It'd have been weird if they hadn't looked at you.'

'You know, the teacher didn't answer me. He just kept looking at me. Do I look stupid? Back at the restaurant, when I was going over the menu with customers, they cocked their heads and weren't happy until they saw me smile.'

'Every novice gets nervous. Just take it slow. There's a first time for everything.'

'Ah, that's what the teacher said. He said that I should learn to walk slowly if I wanted to take good pictures. He was right, of course, and it sounded philosophical, but some people even take pictures from a train, don't they? Walk slowly . . . Hmm, you haven't pointed out any of my shortcomings. Do you think I ought to change, walk and talk more slowly?'

'Have you ever seen a sparrow suddenly slow down and glide like an eagle?'

Outrageous . . . She shrugged and glared at me as her face reddened.

A month later she joined a photographer's hike to a coastal wetland. They stopped at an ancient house in a small town, and saw a tall, reportedly unique cherry tree at the teacher's house. One of the photos showed all the students crowded in among the cherry blossoms. It must have been a cold day, since Qiuzi, who had not dressed warmly enough, shrank back in the middle of the second row, looking shabby and forlorn.

After looking at the pictures, I told her we should go and buy her some new clothes.

She said it was about time to put away her winter clothes, that it didn't feel cold at all.

'So how about it? Do you want to see my first shots or don't you?'

'Wow, I didn't expect you to go through with it. You were afraid they wouldn't be any good.'

Obviously eager to know what I thought, she promptly brought out some photos she'd hidden in a drawer. The first time I saw the cherry tree was in one of her pictures, so I examined each photo carefully with delight. It must have been a Yoshino cherry, a rare species with pink petals surrounding a spot of red in the centre, looking like a cherry tree and a peach tree at the same time.

But, to be honest, I thought the flowers looked bloated in her pictures and that she'd failed to capture the older, hardy branches that extended over the garden wall and disappeared into the narrow borders of the picture frame. Clearly, she'd been hemmed in by the house's surrounding walls.

3

Large-scale land levelling and slope clearing flattened and opened up the craggy hilltops. All the rubbish trees and underbrush were cleared, leaving only deep-rooted native trees scattered along the path; under a canopy formed by rows of mature branches ran an interconnected green belt of vegetation. Pipes buried at the base of the slope connected to a pond where mallards swam among water lilies.

To increase his chances of success, Boss Motor invited agents from a few prominent marketing firms to a briefing. One of them focused on the architect's plans and gave a market appraisal, another suggested changes to the project; the boldest recommendation, from a third firm, was to double the asking price, raising the cost of each unit to a hundred million or more, while insisting on three hundred million for the king of all units, which sat astride the hilltop and had a commanding view of the area.

Having parted on bad terms at the family meeting, members of the Motor clan seemed more agreeable when they heard the proposals – all of them, that is, but their eighty-five-year-old father, who poured cold water on the plans. It was lucky for the clan that he'd made a special trip to join them, for he objected to the jacked-up prices recommended by the third marketing firm that was hoping to get their business. 'The timing is wrong,' he said. 'You all need to think this through. The best price is the one that will move units.'

'They'll pay for the ads, and I don't think they'd waste their own money,' the eldest son said in response.

'It's still better than selling the land, even at a thirty per cent discount. I'm okay with it.' That was the fourth son, who had previously insisted on a land sale.

An ocean of banners flapped in the air. The PR firm hired the month before to represent the clan had made its first moves, slipping an item into several TV news programmes: my Boss Motor, dressed in an Armani suit with a gold-toned bow tie on a white banded collar, all of which he had bought for the taping, stood in the lobby, which was still under construction, and held forth on his youthful dreams: *I've worked like a madman solely for the day when I can retire. Successful entrepreneurs these days are health conscious, hiking in the mountains as often as possible. To me, that's not enough. They should all come here to live . . .*

I heard they'd finally got it right after six takes, and then his secretary spotted a bit of betel nut juice at the corner of his mouth.

The development schedule got tighter as spring was overtaken by summer. For several days, members of the Motor clan were still arguing over the choice of a marketing firm. Only when two companies were left, after a fierce weeding process, did they meet again. To avoid a feud among the three branches of the clan, the sixth son, who had made the long trip from a temple in Kao-hsiung, suggested:

'How about a secret ballot? That'll keep everyone quiet.'

'Why not? With a show of hands we'll just keep on arguing,' one of the elder sons said by way of agreement.

They hadn't realized that eight was an even number until someone downstairs was told to make the ballot slips.

'Our family is stuck with an extra man,' the tech son said, earning a glare from one of the others. Nothing more was said after that. The banners continued to flap outside as dark clouds gathering in the distance dimmed the sky. I stepped up to show the slides once more.

Company A's overall performance and that of the previous year, their latest project, the overall sales rate, and market reviews.

Company B's overall performance and that of the previous year, their latest . . .

A voice interrupted my reading of the statistics:

'You. You're it. I was just thinking that you could be the ninth vote. What do you all think? Number Eight has worked so hard he merits recognition. Let's not argue over this. Giving him an additional vote will count as an extra spur to action.'

Number Eight, my boss, snorted, but his expression gave nothing away. I knew he preferred Company A, whose recommended unit price was the highest, and would add five hundred million in sales for the first phase alone.

It was clearly a gamble. For the first time in my life I witnessed the difference between wealth and money: wealth is built on speculation, unlike money, which can be counted one bill at a time. I felt a chill on my back. The ninth vote was ominous, for it would be a life-or-death matter if the brothers were evenly split. A weighty, critical responsibility was suddenly thrust upon inconsequential me, like putting a flattering top hat on a boil.

The problem was, I didn't like Company A. I'd heard they were into sales gimmicks and often colluded with the media to drive up prices, making it impossible for anyone to buy a unit at the true base price.

I caught a glance from Boss Motor just before the votes were cast. Having lost sleep over the past few days, he was once again suffering from gout. He had limped and shuffled along the slope at noontime. This was my moment to help him and prove my sincerity. The calm gaze in his eyes was a clear sign of his trust in me, for, with my unconditionally loyal vote, his hard work would get him what he wanted.

Sincerity. I liked the word. Like love, it looked pure, leaving no room for doubt. When I cast my sincere vote, the ninth one, dusk was gathering outside, where flocks of birds were chirping.

The voting ended in an incredible five to four, and Company A was out.

A loud buzz erupted in the room, but everything was settled, despite the stunned reactions.

After the other brothers left in their own cars, Boss Motor dragged himself up to the overhang to relieve himself. He didn't turn back straight away, instead seeming to let his gaze linger on the misty distant mountains. Braced with one foot in front of the other, from behind he looked terribly lonely, like a crooked little tree.

Afterwards, I followed him to a restaurant in the foothills, where he ordered a pot of mutton. It was the last pot of the day, and there would be no complimentary refill. The owner said mutton pots wouldn't be on the next day's menu, which was being changed for the new season. The late-spring weather was getting stuffy, and his gout meant that guzzling beer was out of the question, so he ordered a bottle of spirits infused with herbs. Watching his temples turn crimson after only a few sips, I kept my guard up, ready for a grilling. I took small spoonfuls of the broth, all the time wondering what I'd say if he blew up. But he was focused on the food, probably because he knew this was the last of it; with his head down, he gnawed a piece of mutton on the bone, but it was so big and fleshy it slipped and splashed broth all over the table.

He didn't turn his mobile phone back on until we drove back to Taipei. When he finally did, he called the same woman.

'Sure, I know the park. How many this time? I'll go and have a look.'

Yitong Park came into view after I'd circled for a while. The night was sprinkled with a light spring drizzle, the street lamps casting their dreary light through it. Some girls had crowded into a pavilion to shelter from the rain. He told me to stop the car but keep the door closed. Looking out at their faces through the window, he became dispirited. 'My daughter is a high school student in America. She's about their age.'

He took out his mobile phone and cursed whoever was at the other end. *Forget it*, he said.

We backtracked and wound our way out of the park and from there down Jilin Road to the family's private guest house. 'It's getting late. Do you want to spend the night here and go back up the hill tomorrow morning?' he asked me.

'I've got used to sleeping in the clubhouse, waking up at the same time as the singing birds.'

'Well okay, if you're used to it. I know you're a weird guy. One of the girls back there was something else. Just looking at her thighs you could tell she wasn't wearing underwear. Aren't you at all interested in sex? How are you going to spend the rest of your life? And don't tell me you're like a monk when you're away from your wife.'

'I'll think about it next time.'

'Whoring brings men together.'

He got out after that. He was obviously bothered by the vote, but didn't say anything, to my surprise. The mountain road was deserted on my return, and it was quiet on the hill, eerily so. I called Qiuzi. *Our living room is brimming with cut flowers, all leftovers from the florist's. Naturally, they're mostly roses and, can you believe it, several boughs of magnolia with red and white buds. I put them in a vase on your desk. Can you smell them? I'm joking, magnolias have no fragrance . . .*

I did smell gardenias that were finally in bloom, their scent slipping in through the clubhouse rear window. Redolent with the aroma of face powder, it went deeply into my nose, as if I'd buried my face in the blossoms. Mother had planted gardenias when I was five, before the traffic accident; she cut the flowers and put them in vases around the house, their bouquet still lingering in my memory.

I didn't think about Mother often, doing my best to suppress the memory of her when I was sad and preferring to forget her even more when I was happy. Only when I was confronted with an empty feeling, such as at this moment, with the sudden smell of gardenias, would an emptiness overtake Qiuzi's absence and send me adrift in solitude; as I slowly sank into a world of darkness, the image of my mother's face floated into my head. But it was never clear; sometimes it was her shattered face after the accident, but if I was lucky, it would be her smiling as she arranged the gardenias.

That mood kept me up all night. I felt as if I were lying at the top of a mountain, where all the insects and frogs, awakening from their winter hibernation, were chirping and croaking at the top of their voices, the waves of sound pulsating around the flowers.

Clearly I too was bothered by the voting results.

I lost sleep over Boss Motor's reticence about the vote.

4

Company B, which had won the bid by one vote, came to sign the contract the following morning.

It also bought the not-yet-completed clubhouse, thus speeding things up, including the initial sales stage. Within days, the scaffolding for billboards went up all over the hill, while a pair of hired vehicles ferried potential buyers up and down the mountain road, even bringing up hikers taking a break at a hillside tea room.

Who else would you have seen if you hadn't met us?

As an exploratory move, promotional ads were run in the breaks in mainstream films, in print media, on the canvas sides of trucks, and on roadside hoardings, focusing all the advertising firepower on this one line. The phrase was alluring and yet cocky, with a degree of arrogance that meant we were it. It was an ingenious plan, overflowing with bluster, an aggressive opening gambit. From what I had learned, it would surely hit the wealthiest in their most vulnerable spot – that is, their loneliness – but it might also inadvertently hurt the feelings of another group of people who were more understated in their tastes.

The line was packaged in various ways across the different media formats, sometimes in white script on a black background leaping onto TV screens – *ta ta ta*, like machine-gun fire – sometimes showing up unexpectedly on pocket packs of tissues, even appearing on a sky-blocking billboard that towered above a gorge, daily killing scores of hatchlings who, learning to fly, smashed into its bamboo scaffolding.

Company B settled on a forty-day pre-sale period as it worked on the regular ads, while passing tourists came up to take a look. Large parasols opened up on the site for afternoon tea; the aroma of coffee permeated a café in a secluded location in the trees during those days in May. A part-time pastry chef hired from a restaurant in a five-star hotel even provided tableside service, including buttery cannoli with cups of rose tea and caramelized, locally sourced bananas fried in shallow pans.

Each afternoon Boss Motor sat under a newly transplanted cape lilac tree. Banana pancakes were off-limits for him – too much sugar – so he drank two cups of Mandheling coffee instead. When he was bored, he picked up a pair of binoculars to check the progress of the clubhouse construction, sometimes tracking the visitors to see whether they were racing off the hill or taking money out of their pockets.

A month later, he was training his binoculars on a sky recently cleared of rain, taking note of every little thing, including the contrails left by passing aeroplanes.

He asked me what was happening. 'Haven't we sold even one unit?'

I suggested that he train his binoculars on the south-side ridge, for he should be worrying more about the retaining wall that had collapsed during the previous month's unending rain. Following reinforcement work, it now had steel posts sunk deep in the ground, wooden frames that were thicker and wider, and cement that was more than double the amount poured the first time, adding three metres to its height. The emergency work had been done well, but the sight of the towering wall frightened potential buyers, who wondered if it would collapse again one day.

I recommended abandoning the development of the south-side slope so that it wouldn't drag the whole hill down with it.

'You don't realize how solid it is now. Ten trucks couldn't knock it over,' he replied.

I knew more about the previous collapse than anyone because I'd spent my nights at the temporary clubhouse. Looking out from the back window, I could see the forward slope above the retaining wall, a carpet of lush green grass. The startled birdcalls on that fateful night had come as a surprise, as if someone were trying to sneak in through the grove of trees. After the birdcalls came rustling noises, like a swarm of whispering thieves. Their murmured conversation had barely finished when the hilltop began to slide down the slope like cascading sand in a giant hourglass, the mudflow hurtling downward, replete with rocks, as the indestructible retaining wall sank into the black mountain torrent with a boom.

'I hear our competitors are launching attacks on us, saying we're repeating the tragic 1997 collapse of Lincoln Manor.'

'I want those motherfuckers' names.'

After the tourists left, he trained his binoculars back on the sky, but not a single bird was visible.

Ten days went by, and the ads were now out in full force. For three days, they took up entire newspaper pages, drawing stragglers who came up the hill to escape the heat. Boss Motor was on edge. He took himself to the little rooftop garden on the clubhouse, where two temps fetched a large parasol from the warehouse to provide shade for his anxiety. Before they left, he called out to one of them, 'Tell me, Xiaowan. How many visitors do we have down there?'

'A lot,' she said.

'How many is a lot? Are the people clapping in the sales office?'

'We'd like to clap, too, Mr Chairman,' Xiaowan said, shaking her head.

'Then go downstairs and do it. Tell them not to come see me until their hands hurt from clapping.'

It gets dark early in the mountains; when the visitors left at dusk, Boss Motor came down to the lobby, where he paced with his hands behind his back. 'Tell me how you think it went today.' He paused in front of a sales rep, a woman.

'They weren't a good match for us. I'd be more confident if they had been.'

He went over to another rep, a man this time. 'Don't just repeat what she said.'

'They thought the prices were too high, so they didn't want to listen to my sales pitch.'

He then went to the project manager and, after taking a long look at the man, a sentimental tone crept into his voice: 'When I was your age I went by myself to America. One day in the subway, some guy pressed a knife against me while spewing out a torrent of gangster talk, something like, *your money or your life*. I broke his wrist with a couple of quick moves. Want to know how? I couldn't have whipped out a gun in time, even if I'd had one, and I never learned martial arts, so frankly I was scared shitless. But I just started laughing; I laughed so hard I had tears in my eyes. The guy froze, convinced that I'd spotted a weakness in him. That distraction gave me the chance to take him down.'

No one was laughing.

'You look just like that guy, distracted and crestfallen.'

'I see what you mean, Mr Chairman.'

'Your company sounded so bold and impressive when you were here at the briefing. Go and tell your boss to come up with a new strategy. Keep a firm grip on the knife so you won't drop it.'

The unexpected mention of the subway encounter staggered me. He sounded so serious and believable, just the way he looked when he attended funerals. I saw him as a sort of wandering samurai, who had swaggered from one end of the world to the other, saying whatever he wanted, making sense out of nonsense. There must have been a mysterious crack somewhere deep inside him, though I couldn't say what it was or where, only that he'd have been a different person if the crack were mended.

When I got home, I tried the comical subway anecdote on Qiuzi. She didn't laugh either.

'The gangster had lousy luck. At the hospital he was probably still wondering what your boss was laughing about.'

Boss Motor, who couldn't make Qiuzi laugh, reached an agreement with the marketing company more than a month later, pulling all the ads, leaving only two workers to deal with the aftermath, and removing the banners along the ridge. The midsummer days sprawled under a scorching sun, while birds called out shrilly as they took over the bamboo scaffolding that had yet to be removed.

On the evening when the curtain came down on marketing,

he went to lie on the open slope with beer he had sent someone down to buy. By the time I found him, he had fallen off the wagon and polished off three cans. His suffering feet, swollen and ignored, were resting on a pair of slippers. Above, countless stars flickered in the sky, but his eyes were shut; a burnt-down cigarette was clamped between two fingers. It was obvious he'd been there too long to move. He'd suffered a defeat, an ugly defeat, under the relentless onslaught of the ads. His brothers had taken turns sending people up to check on things just about every day, but he had hidden from them, not even coming out to say hello. It was not hard to imagine how the news they took back would get worse by the day.

I soon joined him and tossed down two cans of beer. The stars were so bright that suddenly I felt lost. I'd been working for him for nearly four years, and as I lay beside him on a hill not far from the Xindian River, I wondered if I should congratulate myself for making it this far or get the hell out of this godforsaken place.

I didn't expect him to bring up what had happened at a moment like this.

'That vote of yours, I know you meant it as a reminder to me.'

What could I say? But at least now it was my chance to say to him: weren't the brothers evenly divided? That meant that at least he had the silent support of four of his brothers. They had wanted to help him out, so they'd voted for Company B with the lower bid.

He was tipsy and belched loudly, before bringing up a name.

Luciano Pavarotti.

'Did you ever hear him hit those magical high notes, those

nine consecutive High C's? I looked forward to them every time I went to one of his performances, but they also scared me. I longed to hear them, but couldn't bring myself to listen, afraid he wouldn't make it. Listening to him always made me feel wonderful, though, because it was like he was singing the high notes for my sake. The biggest regret in one's life is failing to make the high note.'

'I've been feeling that regret for a long time.'

'I haven't finished. I wanted to tell you about his father, not him. I read someplace that his old man also had a good voice, but he was so shy he preferred being a baker in the army. A good voice is hereditary, but luckily baking skills are not. Try to imagine a Pavarotti who could not sing and could only bake bread. On the other hand, he would look the part of a baker in an Italian restaurant. With his portly shape and that full beard, he looks like a man who had eaten all the bread he couldn't sell.'

I thought he was drunk.

'I'm like Pavarotti's old man, don't you think?'

'How so?'

'Can't you see I'm shy? Remember, my mother is the third wife. I didn't dare so much as fart when the seven of them ganged up on me. How sad is that! Maybe I was born to be a fucking baker.'

'What a pity. Why didn't his old man come out to fucking sing?'

Pleased that I'd responded, he pushed himself shakily up and asked, 'Want to go down with me?'

I shook my head. He pushed the driver away when he came up to help him.

He rolled down the rear window and stuck his head out.

'Help me out here. Give me an idea what to do next. With such a terrible start, I have no one to turn to. I thought you were an original thinker. At least share some of your damned originality with me – otherwise I could even say that leaving my wife in America was an original idea.'

I waved the driver off into the dark, but Boss Motor sprawled against the window and beckoned for me to come up close, so he could pass some more hot air my way. I listened carefully, ready for him to carry on about high notes, but his mouth was so close all I could hear was a raspy noise. Finally I heard it, a sound so surreal it sent me into a rapturous state.

5

I told Qiuzi all about it when I got home, well past midnight.

As I had expected, she reacted without hesitation when I repeated what Boss Motor had whispered to me, happily sharing my joy.

'My god! He's giving you the whole mountain.'

'Mmm. He wants me to prepare a proposal for the whole clan.'

'But why you?'

'The promotion has failed, and he wants my ideas after suffering this bitter defeat. Actually, I know the terrain and topography better than anyone, but more importantly, I'm completely devoted to the project and emotionally invested in that hill.'

Qiuzi reached up, but this time to wipe away tears rolling down her cheeks, not to cover her face. I hadn't expected her to be so deeply affected, which could only mean she had changed. Learning that her husband was so highly regarded by his superior stirred up tender feelings towards the latter. Was that because we were so frequently separated, though only briefly, or was it because our hearts had never been apart?

Then I brought up something else.

'As an additional gesture of goodwill, he promised that at the family meeting he would ask them to give me a share if they liked my proposal. The decision on how much to invest would be ours, just as it is up to us to decide whether we want to improve our situation at all.'

She stopped crying and asked as she sniffled, 'But where will we get the money?'

'I know. I wish we had it. That's why I didn't bring it up until after I'd told you the good news. It's just a secondary matter, we don't have to invest. But now it's your turn. What did you want to tell me? I could smell it as soon as I opened the door. There's something mysterious in the air whenever you have something to say.'

With a feeble attempt to hide her smile and a coy roll of her eyes, an expression of private joy blossomed on her face. Finally, she produced a stack of photos, and flipped them over, one at a time. 'Don't laugh,' she said, 'please don't laugh at me.' Then she lowered her head to wait for my reaction, eagerly hoping to hear the praise she sought.

She'd photographed the roses in the vase on the table, neighbourhood children, the busy florist, and the park, emptied of visitors, all snapshots, all highlighting her loneliness during my absence. I could tell that the camera had failed to expand her horizons. Instead, her lens had actually exposed the narrow confines of our life.

Naturally, I had to say something nice, for she was still waiting, hands cupping her chin, as if she could wait till dawn. I said, 'Hmm, that's a good angle, beautiful composition, perfect focal distance, Qiuzi, and you captured the charm of the buds . . .'

'Idiot. I included other people's pictures.'

'I really can't tell who shot what, so that means you're doing better.'

Outrageous, mumbled a persistent Qiuzi as she showed me several street scenes, including an alley shot clearly taken from our upstairs window on a rainy night, where a sleek, bright light was reflected off parked cars.

Which was why I immediately agreed to go when she mentioned that we'd been invited out the next day.

Every new place was important to us, since we lived such a constricted life; we wouldn't know how to set sail for the future if we didn't try to expand our horizons. Besides, we were so full of joy, now that she'd discovered a window into photography and I'd finally climbed onto a hilltop that promised abundant hope. What a happy coincidence. When the heavens show concern for a small family like ours, it cannot be a casual act; they must first determine whether we have any dreams, and then slowly fulfil them over time.

And so I finally heard the unfamiliar name for the first time: Luo Yiming.

At first I thought that was the name of a scenic spot; I didn't know it was a man's name, a truly consequential name. A name that would change the course of our lives, the way a river easily swallows up a single drop of water.

But at that moment, how could we have known what the future held? We were too happy to care. Inspirational mottos urge you to grab opportunity like an imperial decree. Yes, an opportunity to expand our horizon had arrived, and this time we were ready to grab it.

'He's the photography class teacher. We took pictures of the cherry blossoms at his house that time.'

'Now I remember. You said he teaches the class for free. You don't come across people like that often.'

Actually, from a certain artistic perspective, Mr Luo Yiming might truly have thought highly of Qiuzi's early shots. Yet I could see that her desire to seek praise from others stemmed from a lack of it in my treatment of her; she might not have been so eager to build up her self-confidence if my love for her had included an appropriate degree of appreciation and approval.

And so I set out the following morning with her on the back of my motor scooter. I was happy, filled with gratitude and joy. Someone had invited her out, which was certainly more satisfying than empty words of love from me; I was even in a hurry to get her there as fast as possible. We sped through a high wind and she held on to me tightly as we made our first outing together since our wedding a year before.

My mental image of Mr Luo Yiming came from the tall cherry tree in her photos, supplemented by details she had supplied from time to time, such as the way he taught the class, the manner in which he gazed at her, the appearance of his old-fashioned family compound, and the look of the veranda made of interlocking boards. In my mind, Luo Yiming was no more than an inverted reflection of Boss Motor in some aspects: he was rich, and he had a huge home and an easy, comfortable life. What was wrong with the two of us? We never actively sought anything on our own initiative, and yet deep down we each seemed to revere an icon. Could that be a result of our lowly, impoverished existence?

So I would be lying if I said I didn't feel a hint of jealousy when I walked through the gate, particularly because the place was as magnificent as I had envisaged. I believed that any house in this town, and indeed any of the opulent mansions that I would see later, paled in comparison. Lucky for us, its owner was unassuming, unlike Boss Motor, who needed his motorcade with two empty cars. Feeling diminished by the imposing residence, I was lost for words and wondered if I should call him Luo Laoshi, Manager Luo, or Mr Luo, the last of which was somewhat vague yet respectful.

He gave me a friendly handshake, his solid, strong fingertips emitting a warm current through the palm. As he led us into the house, the rooms had a slight chill, even in July. I detected the fragrance of sandalwood. Shadows from the shrubbery outside were cast on the white paper pane of a far window. The house felt too big to me. In the soaring space created by walls of untreated wood, our voices practically disappeared into the high ceiling, as though someone eavesdropping from above were sucking away the final syllables.

I was curious to know how many people lived in such a palatial space, and why no one else was in sight. Was he lonely like me when I slept alone in the temporary clubhouse?

He invited us to sit in an elegant room and brought out tea he made himself. After some small talk, Qiuzi produced the photos she'd shown me the night before. Suddenly on edge, I turned my gaze to see what there was in the room and beyond the window, all the while pricking up my ears, afraid Qiuzi might get a negative critique. Any criticism of her would hurt me too; I knew that my emotional frailty was embarrassing, but I couldn't abide anyone putting her down.

Fortunately he didn't criticize her. In his smile was the hint of an appreciative compliment which, though I knew it wasn't necessarily sincere, demonstrated the decency and kindness he retained, despite his accomplishments in the field.

My mind was finally put at ease when an animated discussion got under way between her and the teacher.

Several times over the months that followed, in the period when I was busy working on the hillside proposal, I went with Qiuzi to the Luo house during my free time. Their conversations seldom strayed from photography, which suited me perfectly; we were getting to know each other better, and as their friendship grew, I could let my mind roam free, testing out ideas for the development.

Granted, all three of us were oblivious to one thing.

Why did Miss Baixiu, a college girl at the time, eavesdrop on us? Could she have sensed something?

Ah, Miss Baixiu. Maybe we'd been talking, maybe not, when you stole down the stairs barefoot and then quickly sprang back up, like a cat whose nails would scratch at old wounds years later.

6

A pile of red-skinned sweet potatoes suddenly appeared in the corner of the kitchen. When I came home Qiuzi placed a small clay brazier on the dining table and lit the longan briquettes, slowly infusing the apartment with the aroma of roasted sweet potatoes.

But she remained silent as she worked, which lessened the appeal of the nostalgic scent. Seeing her in such a state always worried me. Her happiness and her sorrow were easy to detect, except when her lips remained pressed together, like now, as she charred the sweet potatoes in the brazier. For her, silence was most unusual.

Luckily, it couldn't last forever; holding something back too long disturbed her fair complexion, causing red and white blotches to erupt, a look she hated. She once told me that people thought she was bashful when actually she was quietly stewing in anger.

Sure enough, she finally spoke up without a prompt, saying she'd gone to her parents' house and bought the sweet potatoes in Zhushan on the way back.

'No one was home. Papa was off tending someone's field and Mama was at work at the processing plant, drying tea leaves. She came home after dark when the leaves were sent to be fried. I knew I shouldn't have gone home. She was startled to see me. *What are you doing here? What's wrong? I'll make you some good-luck rice noodles, but you must go home as soon as you finish.* Outrageous. She treated me like a ghost.'

'She was right. I'm curious as to why you suddenly decided to go back.'

She glanced at me briefly and then looked away, blinking as her eyes reddened. She laid her head on the table.

'In fact, I was the outrageous one. I actually asked her about the price of bamboo. That surprised her. My younger brother came home a while later. He's found a job working for somebody now he's out of the military. His hand was bandaged. When he walked me to bus stop, he said, "Don't worry, sis. After next month I won't be an apprentice any longer, and you can have all the money from bamboo sales."'

'So you went home to borrow money.'

'I'd already asked everyone else. As soon as they hear what I'm after, they tell me how badly off they are.'

'What I mentioned to you, that's over and done with,' I said lightly.

I'd been so emotional on our wedding day, when the five of us silently shared that seafood dinner and I'd promised to treat Qiuzi well. Now, as I thought back, I felt a demoralizing sadness. I'd put her under too much pressure. I shouldn't have spoken of investing in the project, since it was beyond our financial means, and although she'd said nothing, it had been on her mind ever since.

Maybe she'd seen the look of disappointment on my face,

and that had led to her foolish decision to try to help. I suddenly realized how quiet I'd been around her for months. Devoting all my attention to the proposal could have been one of the reasons, but in fact there was a demonic image gnawing at me. Each time I left Luo's big house I did so in a state of melancholy, a feeling akin to the indescribable and unfathomable bleakness I'd felt when I'd followed Boss Motor's mini motorcade on my scooter.

Of course I knew what it was. I was still spellbound by the aura of power that symbolized prestige, and, sad to say, I had no intention of breaking free; I was dogged by its eerie presence. What I actually wanted to be free of was my father, who had caused me anguish even as I'd climbed out from under the shadow of his tragedy. I wanted to step away, far enough away to forget him completely, but sometimes I found myself hurled back to where I'd started. Luo Yiming and Boss Motor made me aware of my lowly origins.

Behind the brazier, a vase of ginger lilies caught my eye.

I ate two charred, unpeeled sweet potatoes, filling my mouth with the bitter taste of charcoal. Father and I had once built a clay oven in our neighbour's field. Father had gathered rice stalks while I built the oven by piling up dirt clods, after which we tossed in the burning stalks. Then we smashed the clods, covering the sweet potatoes and roasting them. Father lit a cigarette as we sat waiting on a furrowed ridge. As far as I can recall, that cool post-harvest afternoon was the most delightful scene in his short life; he walked into a deep spot in the stream less than six months later.

I hadn't said anything to Qiuzi up to now about roasting sweet potatoes with Father, because of its eventual tragic ending. Of course I could have, as long as I'd omitted the final part. How wonderful everything in life could be without endings; a story that stops before it is over is like wings of happiness beating in mid-air with no fear of falling.

She'd heard my story about the sticky rice balls over the winter solstice. I'd erased the ending, leaving in her mind only the image of rice balls on the floor. The way we'd laughed as we picked them up and put them in our mouths was hilarious to her. It made sense that she would want to know why I'd had to bite them in half, since I'd never previously told her about Mother's debilitating injury.

So I told her about roasting sweet potatoes the same way. *Qiuzi, I love charred sweet potatoes, it's the only way to roast them. They're tastiest when they're burned black as the ashes in a clay oven. When we dug out the potatoes, Father and I kept rubbing off the ashes until our faces were so black only our teeth showed. Can you imagine how thrilling those potatoes were? That's the only way to eat them.*

This time she didn't say, *And then?*

It seems nothing about my life can be told from start to finish. It was getting dark when Father and I left the field. Mother was waiting for us to come home and turn on the light. And then? And then the sky turned pitch black, so dark it seemed boundless; it flooded my mind for a seeming eternity.

7

The hill on the northeast corner stretched out across open terrain in the morning light. The topsoil had a serene and pleasant coolness after an overnight sprinkling of dew. Birds had yet to take wing and butterflies and dragonflies still rested on trees. A watery patina covered rocks stacked along the winding slope. Recently dug out of the ground, they seemed eager to stretch as they quietly shed a coat of dirt; autumn frost from the night before flickered on their rust-coloured cut sides.

I could see from this vantage point that the city of Taipei still slumbered in its basin.

I turned to look at the southern plot, which lay at the bottom of the forward slope. It was a fairly large, smooth section of land that had been chiselled out of rocky crags, with a new retaining wall that rose above the treetops. Soon small detached houses would appear there, competing with heaven for space and putting their fate in the hands of the wind and rain, light or heavy.

I recorded everything for my presentation, while at the same time checking the gaps between rocks, looking into all the drainage ditches and taking pictures of sections of netting. To be sure, no matter how carefully I kept track of it all, a single rainstorm could make all my observations irrelevant. I had been plagued by nagging concerns for days and I kept applying pressure on Boss Motor.

'The hill will look less spoiled if we refrain from developing the south slope.'

'Even if I agreed with you, we would still face seven opinionated mouths.'

'You yourself said you wanted to sing that last High C.'

'Why don't you tell me how to sing it first? I'll talk to them only if I'm armed with good ideas from you.'

He called each of them the next day despite what he'd said, and as he'd predicted, the seven mouths were argument-ative as well as articulate. A few even shouted so loudly that he had to cover his ears and keep talking, turning the call into an auditory battle.

He wore a dark, angry look as he told someone to schedule a meeting to resolve the issue. He was willing to take a chance on my suggestion, but would give up and let the hill return to nature if the others objected.

After a series of back and forth messages, they settled on an afternoon ten days later for the presentation.

Shortly past noon on the stipulated day, luxury sedans drove up the mountain road. All seven brothers came alone, more or less, and none of them arrived with greetings or a willingness to chat, as if a bitter fight between martial arts masters was about to take place. Boss Motor and I were sit-ting on the clubhouse roof eating packed lunches. He kept glancing below and finally laid down his chopsticks. 'Look at that fat one. He's a temple overseer, and yet still he can make it here for the presentation. As a devout believer, he's the one who's least afraid of landslides. The others aren't any better. People are always saying you win only through hard work, and brothers unite as one, but that's bullshit. They all want to get a piece of this treasure mountain. They haven't come in the spirit of goodwill.'

Then he pressed me with, 'How can you sit there and enjoy your lunch like that? Go and get ready. Make sure those guys don't run off before you're halfway through.'

'I'll try to keep you out of it.'

'Is everything ready?'

'Yes, my suitcase is packed,' I replied with a laugh.

Proposal: The story of the floodway ponds.

Concept: An affecting mountain.

Appeal: Non-moneyed, social idealism, business with conscience.

Scale: smaller in size, larger in opportunity, look towards hope.

I walked up to the podium and bowed to show my respect before turning to the slide projection on the wall and silently reading the script for twenty seconds. Then I greeted them. I didn't know them well. Except for number six, the temple overseer, they were all pillars of society. So I introduced myself, told them my name, my length of employment, and the reason for my presence before them.

I began with the failed sales proposal from three months before: *Well, it wasn't a real failure, it's just that we were in such a hurry we forgot to give the mountain a unique life story, a name it deserves, and a dream for the future. We thought only luxury* mansions could enrich a mountain, but that experience has taught us that a mountain can be enriched purely by its own life, just as happems in our society, where those who pursue hope can bring us hope, not only the rich.

'No need to preach,' said the temple overseer.

Good point. I never did like preaching. I looked past the circle of light above his head as I projected five colour photos onto the wall, one at a time. All were of floodway ponds, taken a few days earlier, in the brief moments of morning light. Summer rain filled these ponds, which were the size of basketball courts, their surfaces reflecting the lush green of the slopes and, in the centres, puffs of cottony clouds.

I want to tell you about these ponds. We don't think much about them and we've simply followed regulations that require them for water drainage and flood control. I'm sorry, but they are the focus of my proposal today, and I want them to tell a complete story.

Worried that I might be straining their patience, I began to read the script:

The protagonist of this story is an old man.

The first pond: let us imagine a boat on the slope, and that he's fishing in the boat.

The second pond: he has finally caught a fish, but it is too big for him to handle, a super fish.

The third pond: the big fish fights to get free, and the old man sustains a serious injury and falls to the bottom of the boat.

The fourth pond: the big fish floats to the surface a few days later; the old man is exhausted.

The fifth pond: a fish skeleton, intact from head to tail, lies in the boat, and the old man returns to port.

*

When, finally, someone voiced a question, I knew we were getting somewhere.

'You made that story up, didn't you? What's the point?'

'It's Hemingway's *The Old Man and the Sea*. I divided the story into five segments.'

'Let's hear him out, since we're here anyway,' one of them turned and said to the others.

So I continued, 'It is serendipitous that we have five floodway ponds here. We can imagine them as lakes or an ocean in our life. In my attempt to create an inspirational narrative for the mountain, I started out with the story in Hemingway's novel, hoping to motivate the younger generation and turn this area into an ideal site for an outdoor classroom. Teachers from all over the island can bring their students, and parents can come with their children to learn and understand from these al fresco sculptures the meaning of an old man fighting the sea. But later I realized that the function I'd envisaged was too narrow, and that the spirit of the story could be broadened. Or, put differently, every person could be a reading guide for him or herself. A man would see the struggle he goes through in life; young people would learn about their potential from the effort. We can all be the interpreters of this site and this scene. Even a failure can learn from the old man and appreciate anew the endless possibilities in life.'

'But in the end he failed, and took home only a fish skeleton,' one of them said.

'You're right about that, but it wasn't the only possible outcome. He had leg cramps, he lost control of his hands, his torn shoulder started to fester, and he was coughing up blood. He could have returned home safe and sound but empty-handed if he'd cut loose the fishing line over his shoulder. To me, therein lies a person's greatest value. The marlin – I'm sorry, I forgot to tell you it's a marlin – the unyielding marlin was beyond the old man's ability to fight with, but he continued with the failed struggle to triumph over himself. And that's where Hemingway's famous line came from – a man can be destroyed but not defeated.'

'Even if there's some ridiculous value in it, what does it have to do with your proposal?' one of them cut in.

'I think this is an opportunity to give the mountain its own identity. Our social values have long been compromised. A mountain villa is always associated with the nobility or the super rich, while in fact most wealthy people are manifestations of society's ruthless nature. Why don't we seize this opportunity to reduce the size of the luxury units, which in turn will give more people hope? If it strikes a chord with enough of them, others will follow our example wherever they may be. Only with this vision will our children dare to grow up and our young people dare to look forward to the future. If opportunity abounds, then hope will exist everywhere, sort of like what the old man says – "If good luck is sold somewhere, I'd like to buy some of it."'

'So you're suggesting that we sell at a lower price?'

'Of course there will have to be a careful calculation. But we can save considerable resources and capital by not stressing the luxury aspect, and the sales price will be attractive and approachable. Besides, we've planned for a school, a market, a park and a commercial street. I believe that a small mountain town like that would be very appealing. That's the kind of value system I'd like to present, one that can enrich the life of the mountain.'

After recovering from a stunned silence, the brothers

began talking among themselves, as if they'd found a lost connection to one another.

All but my boss, the youngest son. Looking grave, he leaned back in his chair, arms folded across his chest. I thought he might be mulling it over and wasn't yet ready to show his happiness. I wondered if he knew that I had struggled to come up with this idea, that it had in fact been inspired by the night we'd drunk beer together. I wanted to help soothe his parched throat so he could finally produce the High C he'd hoped for. I was convinced that if my proposal failed to pass, the mountain would be overgrown with weeds and would stay that way for a very long time, just as he said. And he would never again be able to raise his head in the presence of his brothers. No matter what high note he wanted to sing among them, even the lowest note would stick in his throat.

Sincerity. Still one of my favourite words, along with love.

Undeniably, my sincerity was mixed with musical notes thumping somewhere deep inside my heart. I was sincere with myself, and with Qiuzi. Sometimes I was reminded of those desolate figures lying in the middle of Zhongxiao East Road. Sometimes I thought about Mother, too. I only recalled Father when I couldn't help myself, for even though I was in his debt, I hated him. No one knew why I'd thought about Hemingway. I'd read *The Old Man and the Sea* not because I liked tragic stories, but because there was a connection between the old man and me, an emotional tie that Father could not have given me.

The presentation had been halted by the discussion among the brothers. Boss Motor had remained silent, I noted. I supposed he was afraid, for he was often lost in a puzzling contemplation that stemmed from a lack of self-confidence.

He seemed to be suffering from stage fright at this inopportune moment, when he should have been joining in with his brothers in their animated discussion. His timidity sprang from a dark spot in his heart, a result of his lowly origin as the son of the third wife.

The oldest son was the first to speak once the room was quiet again.

'We've talked it over and agree that your proposal isn't bad. Storytelling is fashionable in this consumer-culture age. You told a very good story, but we mustn't forget that idealism is only fine as long as we can make a profit.'

'I know. We can increase the number of units without exceeding the limit set during the application review. After making a rough calculation of the sales price, I believe we should make a decent profit.'

'Tell us what you think, Old Eight. Will it work?'

'I'm fine as long as you're happy with it.'

The clear-headed temple overseer asked:

'Why should we believe that this is the right path?'

'Half of our success is all but guaranteed if we make sure that no other builder comes to ruin the mountain.'

'Should we keep the original project name?'

'No. It has to be changed.'

'To what?'

I took a deep breath. 'The project will be called "The Old Man and the Sea."'

8

An artist showed up two days later in the afternoon. He came down the path on the slope and through a stand of trees with several others to photograph the floodway ponds from various angles. He had been invited by the fifth brother, the one in tech, who had stayed quiet during the presentation but later brought the artist over for an on-site study, even asking about the possibility of creating a sculpture of an old man fishing.

Like the other sons, No. 5 rarely had any contact with my boss, No. 8. I had met him a few times, but, before today, only during tense family feuds. Now, finally, he struck up a conversation with me as we walked along behind the camera. 'I spent a whole night thinking about your proposal. To be frank, your idea is highly traditional and backward, counter to trends in modern technology. But bringing literature into architecture can be endearing, and it could uplift people. It could even be a terrific selling point. But don't celebrate yet, not everyone is in your corner.'

Boss Motor was trailing behind us. When his brothers were around, he usually hid behind a cloud of smoke, puffing furiously on a cigarette. The longer he remained quiet, the longer would be the monologue that would spill out of him after the crowd departed.

They were about to leave, having discussed materials for the sculpture. I placed two copies of *The Old Man and the Sea* in the fifth brother's car. He stuck his head out through the window and said, 'No one should wait till his fifties to read this. I didn't, but I'll read it again.'

Okay. Remaining faithful to his arrogant personality and lowborn background, Boss Motor looked away, refusing to see the visitors off. He watched me come up the hill and, when I reached him, directed his voice at the disappearing car: 'What bullshit did he just give you?'

'He reminded me not to celebrate too soon.'

'Well, at least he didn't object. He and I had a fistfight before I went into the military. It looks like he's okay now.'

He glanced at his watch and, as he pulled his trench coat tighter around his body, told me to accompany him down the hill.

'With this weather, mutton pots should be back on again.'

We were waiting to hear what the seven brothers had decided. They had exchanged looks after my presentation that day, but the atmosphere had remained cordial, leaving space for our imagination to flourish. But my boss was still worried. He made some calls to the main office without looking for anyone in particular; instead, he spoke to all the department heads, one at a time, and asked all sorts of questions. But he still couldn't get a sense of what his brothers were thinking, so he hung up.

I got a feeling that, in his worried state, he'd likely want me to accompany him to that place.

'Want to go to Yitong Park for mutton pot?'

'You don't have to go to the same place every time for that.'

It was warmer down below, but a December wind reigned on the quiet street corner, so we sat at a table sheltered by a floor-length canvas. When the drinks arrived, he put his feet up and downed half a glass. I envied his casual, carefree style, so unpretentious and rough-hewn, not the sort of person I'd ever thought I'd work for. And yet I'd grown used to this kind of life. Maybe I'd have been more reserved and subservient in front of other people if he'd been more polished. I ought to have considered myself lucky, but I could never be as forthright as he was.

'Come on, drink up. What's going on in that head of yours now?'

'I was just thinking about how the old man finally caught his marlin, but that it was devoured by sharks. Hemingway must have planned for the marlin to be eaten before he started writing the novel. He seemed to be saying that tragedy alone can bring out a person's true worth, but I don't think this should be the only way to value one's life.'

'Honestly, I was sweating bullets watching your present-ation that day. My brothers are a motley crew, and I wonder if they understand Hemingway at all. But suddenly they were all ears, pretending to be learned men, so of course I was flab-bergasted. I thought they were play-acting, but now they clearly seem to be enjoying their roles in the drama. So why don't you tell me what you have in mind? I need to know so that I can help, even if that means completely falling out with them.'

I told him what I was thinking and mentioned the Shell-less Snail Movement during my first days as a civilian. 'They were all older than I am now, but their children have grown up into a new generation of shell-less snails.'

'What does that have to do with the old fisherman?'

'We're all future old men. Are we going to wait till we're old and feeble to seek the value of life? Why can't we create a different sort of value system now, doing our best to treat people better and contributing to society, instead of always promoting luxury mansions? The rich have benefited too much from society already, and we should stop catering to their tastes.'

'You should run for President.'

'Doing this thing well makes me happier than you people get when you make a bundle of money.'

'You're quite the chatterbox today. You should be like this every day – sharing your innermost thoughts can cheer a chap up. Don't think I can't tell that these ideas of yours came from somewhere. I don't know how rough your childhood was, but I sensed something the day you asked for leave to get married. Most people can't contain their joy before their wedding, but not you, you looked as if the sky were falling. How can anyone have such a hangdog look when he's getting married?'

'I vowed that for the rest of our life together, I would give Qiuzi happy surprises as often as possible.'

'Happy surprises? What makes a happy surprise?'

'You wouldn't understand. There can be a happy surprise even in the tiniest of tiny things.'

'Don't try to stump me. Give me an example. How bloody small are we talking?'

'Something only a nobody can have.'

I put a piece of mutton into my mouth to stop the conversation. It was so big my cheeks bulged until they pulled

my eyes out of shape and blurred my vision. It felt hot. I heard
him squawk into his mobile phone, making a dreary, mournful noise that filled my ears like a cicada's chirps. I stuck
a chopstick into my mouth to shift the meaty bone, easing
the uncomfortable, stuffy feeling. My vision cleared when the
tears fell.

He belched, obviously having made arrangements with
the woman.

Sometimes I wished I could be like him, a man with few
worries. When pressures built up, he found a woman, took off
his trousers, and was an entrepreneur again when he put them
back on. If Qiuzi hadn't been in my life, or, put differently, if
she'd never existed, I should probably go to one of those places
to take off my trousers too. No big deal, really. I'd take off
mine, and she'd take off hers. But when would I ever do
something like that? Why would I want to get naked in front
of a woman who was not Qiuzi?

He drained his cup and wiped his mouth. 'Take me there
and you can drive on back.'

'I'll go with you, and then I'll take you back to the guest
house.'

'Now you're scaring me. Are you finally going to have a
taste tonight, or—'

'I just want to see who takes your fancy. That should be
exciting enough for me. I used to play a game when I was in
elementary school. I'd squat by the door at home any time I
heard footsteps in the alley, and even though I knew we never
had visitors, I'd peek through a crack, as if that would make
Father stroll back in.'

'What would your mother say, *Hurry up and open the door,
you idiot?*'

'No, she'd ignore me and stay upstairs clipping her nails.'

Luckily, I wasn't drunk, so I *sincerely* managed to pull the wool over his eyes.

As we entered downtown, he led me through a maze, taking us to Xinyi Road, before circling out of Tonghua Street. He wasn't sure how to get to where he'd been the other time. When I stopped to park, we were in front of a large electronics store. We went up to the second floor, where there was a sign for some kind of club on one of the doors. The room had a very low ceiling and was carpeted in red from one end to the other, as if it was floating on the surface of the sea.

A waiter brought us cups of hot tea before we could order anything, while two young women emerged from behind a row of indoor palm trees and glided gracefully over to a nearby table. Boss Motor sized them up, as if appreciating a painting. I glanced over his shoulder, past some planters, and actually spotted Qiuzi. My Qiuzi! The girl in the shadowy glassed-off booth in the rear of the hall looked exactly like her.

'I'll call her over,' the waiter said.

I could have been wrong, but now the woman was getting up. She had a nearly identical figure and the same long, thin face, but hers was framed by shoulder-length hair. She walked slowly towards me and stopped when she reached the planters, close enough for a better look at her face, though her body was mostly hidden behind the palm leaves, as if to help me hold on to this mistaken identity. I knew she was not Qiuzi and yet I was captivated. Was that because Qiuzi was forever on my mind or because she was omnipresent to the degree that anyone could easily assume her identity to tease and embarrass me?

'Someone you know?' Boss Motor asked. 'Just don't look at her face. You're not doing the face.'

But it wouldn't be Qiuzi if I didn't look at her face, would it?

It was very late when I got back to the mountain, but I called Qiuzi anyway to tell her about the proposal's glimmer of hope. She started to cry, and to me those sobs were heartwarming. I felt especially close to her even though we were not talking face to face. I knew she hadn't been sleeping well, always waiting for any news I might bring her.

'You will be helping lots of people if your proposal is accepted.'

Bringing up the investment money again, she said she'd try to borrow some from her friends and family the next day, since the bamboo had fetched only two hundred thousand NT at year's end. I said, 'Qiuzi, we have to aim higher than that. We'd be worth less than a bamboo shoot if we accepted hardearned money from your family.'

She mumbled her agreement over and over. 'Hmm, I know we shouldn't, but then what are you going to do?'

I said, 'It's all right. It won't kill us if we don't invest in the project. And I'm in a really good mood. I had a bit to drink and I saw someone who looked just like you. I would have called out your name if she hadn't had long hair.'

'Wait until you're home. Don't let anyone hear you,' she said.

9

Spring crept up on the deciduous trees, releasing tender green buds on bare branches all over the hill; red bauhinia and African tulips were blooming all along the ridge. With a suggestion from some of the brothers, the stiff-sounding 'floodway ponds' were renamed 'eco-ponds', a reflection of the lush landscape of the slope. Fireflies appeared earlier than usual. The children of the Motor clan didn't want to go home after a day of flying their kites; they hid behind trees clutching nets instead, waiting for the flickering dots of light to drift out of the darkness.

Once the seven brothers had done with setting up meetings, they brought friends up for hikes, leading contingents to look at the fish in the eco-ponds while promoting the planning concept of 'The Old Man and the Sea'. Most impressive among them was the renowned brain surgeon, a brother whose name I didn't know. Normally a quiet man who liked to tug on his stern, haughty white chin whiskers, on this day he was battling with an imaginary fishing line, exaggerating his movements until he fell backwards and drew riotous laughter from his friends.

As the idea of 'The Old Man and the Sea' began to ferment, it engendered an almost spiritual appeal, in the same way that listeners at a fireside poetry reading go quiet, as clamour dissolves into whispers and old enemies turn into best friends. Something odd was also happening to No. 8, who now tended to smile at his brothers, though from a distance. Afraid they might doubt his sincerity, he inched closer to their small circle, where he stood warily and had the staff set up a long table on the grass and slip light yellow seat covers over a dozen chairs. From behind it had the appearance of a school parents' evening, which would get under way as soon as the lonely silhouettes of the Motor clan appeared.

Everything seemed to be improving at once, including Qiuzi, who had good news to share. Speechless from excitement, she was almost gasping into the phone; finally, I was able to deduce that it had something to do with money. Her photography teacher, Luo Yiming, the bank manager, had surprised her with an offer to lend us the money on a credit loan without collateral.

I'd long since given up hope of investing in a share, but now it was as if a setting sun had started to rise again. There was no reason to put it off, now that someone had extended a helping hand, so I raced down the hill that very night, caught the last bus home, and confirmed our personal information with the bank the next day.

It was all so unexpected – an unexpected reconciliation of the brothers, and an unexpected personal loan. There ought to be even more welcome surprises to come; at least that's what I believed. It would be like springtime, when peach blossoms follow plum flowers and signs of budding life are everywhere. It was a miracle, just like the day I met Qiuzi. If I hadn't walked into the jam store, the thread of inspiration wouldn't have drifted into my head, and there would have been no encounter a few minutes later in the coffee shop.

There would indeed be a surprise, but it turned out to be a black March.

The World Health Organization issued an abrupt warning that a rare respiratory epidemic was spreading in many parts of the world. The first case in Taiwan surfaced several days later, but it was too early to cause a panic. Panicky reactions are usually caused by a surprise gathering, like demonic spectral hands that knock on doors, one after another, on slumbering dark nights. The atmosphere of terror had yet to unfold, and visitors continued to slip into the construction site, where the hills, viewed from afar, seemed rouged by the bewitchingly vivid reds of the African tulips.

But April brought a shock. Several cases of infection were found in Taipei's Heping Hospital, which was immediately sealed off, and streets suspected of contamination were barricaded at both ends, as fear began to spread. People wore masks when they went out, sometimes even when they stayed home. They couldn't turn on their TV sets without being blasted by news of the epidemic. Television stations parked their news-broadcasting vans outside the hospital and trained their cameras on the window of a special medical team, capturing the staff's eyes, the only parts that were not shielded by HazMat suits.

Cotton trees finished blooming and dropped their petals before the spring was over, after which the uneasiness of early summer settled in and dominated life. I heard that public places, such as restaurants and cinemas, were deserted. The quiet streets were all anyone talked about when they returned to the office after doing errands in town. Boss Motor didn't come to work for six straight days, so the office sent an assistant to the Jilin Road guest house, where, like an orderly, she took his temperature every two hours. The results she sent back stated that he was in perfect health, except that he couldn't walk. His feet were so swollen he kept them on ice pillows and screamed in pain if he had to turn over.

Once his gout improved, he asked about the depressed market, suddenly struck by the idea of going to Taichung.

'Where else can we go these days? It's awful. On my way out of the house, I got into a lift and some bloke sneezed right in my face, thinking he could do what he damn well pleased since he was wearing a mask. How's this for a plan? Drive me back to my family home, and we can just take in the sights. Ask that Qiuzi of yours to join us for dinner. I'd like to meet her and see what she looks like. What do you say? I'll find a restaurant that bans sneezing.'

There were visibly fewer cars on the highway and it was plain sailing after passing Taoyuan. I normally took the train home. Rarely did my foot find an opportunity to step on the gas. A trip home, at such short notice. The car tore down the highway, keeping pace with my thumping heart. I hadn't warned Qiuzi, but why should I? Our life had always followed a schedule, but not on this day, when we had been given a gift of leisure by the heavens, in much the same way a guileless Qiuzi had won an expensive camera.

What a surprised look she'd wear when she opened the door to see me show up unannounced. Just imagining the scene had me speed up as we shot past the sign for Houli.

After dropping off Boss Motor at his family compound, I drove his car down streets I'd ridden through on my motor scooter barely two years earlier. I crossed Wenxin Road and, taking every turn at speed, headed straight for home.

Intending to play a practical joke on her, I put on a surgical mask before pressing the doorbell. I wanted to see her appear confused and uneasy at encountering a stranger, then hesitantly discover that the drifter was her husband who was used to coming home late at night. It would be a terrific surprise for her to see me when she least expected to.

But no one answered the door, though I rang the bell repeatedly.

I let myself in, raced to the bedroom, and then went back to the living room. I was the confused one, as I stood dazed in a surreal space. I called the florist, the photography class and the photo studio she frequented; I even tried her friends, until dusk descended, swallowing up every corner of the house in darkness. My courage to turn on the light had left me by then; all I could manage to do was lay my head on the table to avoid any ray of light that could mire me in more darkness.

I was able to cancel the dinner with Boss Motor that night, but I was afraid the cancellation would be permanent. All through the night, until early morning, I stayed away from the bedroom and forced my stiff limbs to remain in the chair, even when dawn arrived to slowly lighten up the sky.

In the end, I had to rouse myself from my wakefulness. I supposed that sooner or later Qiuzi would let on what had happened. Not wishing to put her in an awkward position, I rearranged everything I had touched to erase signs of my presence and pushed the dining chair back under the table before locking the door and quietly departing.

Like a guilty man on the run, I drove to the old family

compound and waited outside for Boss Motor, so we could return to the north.

The first thing I did when I was back on the mountain was call. She was at home. She didn't mention her night away, just as I said nothing about having shown up unannounced. With the phone at my ear, I couldn't read her silence; it was as if she were a stranger who had happened to walk by, hear a ringing phone, pick it up, and then lay it down.

We'd never been like that before. I didn't dare ask any questions, for fear of causing harm, but silence wasn't an option either. So I said, 'Qiuzi, make sure to wear a mask. The shop is close by, but the virus can be carried on the pollen.' I added, 'I finally saw a barbet the day before yesterday. A super pretty one. It flew out from the treetops and took off when it saw me.'

Her silence was totally out of character, and I began to stammer.

Then she said drily, in a voice with no emotion, 'The loan was approved today.'

10

Two days later, a Friday, mature plum trees were trucked in from outside and planted in waiting holes. As usual, I stood by the crane to watch and help guide the movement of the trees, oblivious to the dead branches hidden among the green leaves, until suddenly one cracked in mid-air, the broken end of a limb, shaped like a catapult, slicing down on me.

The dead limb was denuded, but like a swarm of apparitions, it was impossible to dodge; it ripped through my shirt, bruising my chest. Boss Motor heard of the accident from the foreman of the gardening crew when he came to work in the afternoon, but he didn't mention it, saying only, 'Go on home and take care of your personal business.'

On the bus ride home, I felt a sharp pain deep inside, beyond the bruise.

I usually came home much later on my days off. As I neared the door, I felt strangely timid, momentarily seized by a fear that it would be a repeat of a few days earlier. I hesitated at the daunting threshold, afraid that I would walk straight into a dismal void.

Fortunately, she was home. She heard the doorbell and skipped over, pausing in the hall to put on her slippers. She turned on the outside light and called, Who is it? Who's there? The sound of her voice depressed me. I replied in a tone induced by the sharp pain, a sound so deep it startled even me. Suddenly realizing that I should act normally, I coughed dryly a time or two while waiting for the door to open.

She had recovered her crisp, clear voice. She gave me a customary hug, attempting to bridge the distance created by the phone call. I followed her inside and saw a bowl on the table next to a plate of leftover vegetables from lunch. Obviously she was, as always, eating a dinner she'd just thrown together. But her mind had been elsewhere; photos were spread out on the table, and she hadn't turned on the TV, a favourite pastime of hers.

'Go and have a shower and I'll make something for you.'

Qiuzi had forgotten one thing. No, in fact, she'd abandoned herself.

She was not pleasantly surprised.

For her, this was the first time I'd come home early and unexpectedly, but she acted as if it was as normal as my late-night returns.

After taking out some vegetables from the refrigerator, she turned on the tap to wash them, the sound of running water loud and urgent, as if to scour away every bit of residue. Her short hair, seen from behind, was untidy; the tips curled slightly under her ears, and there were some loose strands. I turned to check the corner of the kitchen, where we stored vegetables. I saw no trace of what would normally be there after one of her visits back home, such as greens or beans when it wasn't bamboo season. Obviously she hadn't gone home two days before. The one path I might have missed came to a dead end.

So, where could she have been?

As the food cooked on the stove, she was suddenly reminded of the photos and, as if to cover something up, she dried her hands and walked over to put them away, so unlike the Quizi of the past, who'd blushed as she'd eagerly showed off her new work. I'd caught a fleeting glance of towering mountains or a solitary peak on photo paper that seemed to have just emerged from a darkroom, with a glare reminiscent of the starlight on the night she'd gone missing.

And so I held out my hand.

She hesitated, stiff and uncertain at first, but then handed me the photos and walked away.

The thick stack of photos depicted mountains where birds had flown off, like the line from a Tang poem. *A sea of clouds hanging above met a pristine, empty wilderness.* It was a dreamscape we'd never visited, of that I was certain, and even the mountain I walked on every day didn't offer such a secluded, serene view. She had captured a lone pine on a craggy cliff, its twisted branches stretching into the clouds, where the verdant fir trees thrived in the heavy chill of the high altitude.

Qiuzi had evidently managed to leave the narrow confines of her daily routine, but she had gone too far.

Actually, I wanted to hear her say something, anything. I waited for her to come and lean against me and point to the pictures, looking happy and uncertain, as she had before, saying her finger had slipped when she took this one and someone had walked by when she was taking that one – *Just hurry off, would you? I was so anxious I pressed the shutter too soon.*

Of course, to spare me any wild speculative thoughts I

wanted to hear an honest confession and learn the details, maybe where the mountain was located, how many participants there were in the photographic hike, how the site had been too far for her to return home on the same day . . . and, what else? Did Luo Yiming happen to have had the day off?

I could no longer see Qiuzi, although she was standing right in front of me. It was as if she hadn't come home. A long time passed before I came out of the bathroom and pushed her down onto the bed, but I still seemed not to have found her. She had a bathrobe on over her nightgown, and a pair of cotton sweatpants she wore for morning runs in the winter, leaving only her face uncovered. I grabbed the hem of her robe, but the more impatient I was, the stiffer her body grew, as if it had already been soiled and damaged, as if her blood had congealed in the memory of terror.

I ripped the wrapping off her, as though I was tearing open a package.

Ignoring her struggle, I tore off her shoulder straps and stripped her until her upper body was exposed, her injured breast quivering. I panicked and froze. We'd never been like this before. I had always been protective of the breast and had never neglected it, even on those times when we were horsing around and it nearly came into view. Keeping in mind the sorrow behind the injury, I had often glanced at it, a glance rooted in respect and compassion, in love.

But now I'd frightened it.

She stopped squirming and lay there calmly, exposing her body under the white lamplight. She'd forgotten to cover it; or more likely, she didn't feel like shielding it any longer. The scar on the side of her breast was like an innocent child lying next to her, as if a forlorn mother and daughter were waiting for me to cool down from my brutish behaviour.

Nothing happened after that. When I changed into my pyjamas and lay down, she gently pulled the thin blanket up to her mouth, leaving only her teary eyes visible.

I was unaware that a major change had occurred. I don't know how much time passed, but it must have been really late when I drifted into a fitful sleep, well past midnight. I heard her quietly moving about in the dark, making so little noise that it was virtually soundless, like two teeth of a zip being pulled together every ten seconds, or a puff of cotton flying over and drifting away. Then she tiptoed out of the bedroom, opened the front door as if going out to buy soy milk early in the morning, and gently closed it behind her, shutting me inside in a confused state of semi-wakefulness, tears in my eyes.

11

My last image of Qiuzi, it turned out, was of her exposed body that night.

I thought she had gone out for a walk in the park, to a breakfast shop to wait for fresh thin pancakes, or to a convenience store to write a letter at one of their tables. Whether it was to express a sense of guilt or to defend herself, she would quietly hand the letter to me in the morning, the afternoon, or the early evening, leave it at our loving dining table, insert it in a book she was reading, or let me discover it at the head of the bed by turning over casually.

When I could wait no longer to catch a train up north, I left her a note on the dining table. Once I was back on the hill, I rang her incessantly, from late that night to early the next morning, but the unanswered phone calls turned into painful auditory hallucination. I heard the ringing everywhere, inside and outside the room, like unstoppable, frenzied footsteps.

Only two routes were open to me that day. One was the florist's, but she hadn't shown up for work. The second and final one was her family. I thought that that surely would be the place where I'd find her. Her father picked up the phone and barely recognized my voice. He wondered why I'd suddenly thought of them. *Are you two all right? Thinking about coming back for a visit?* Not knowing what to say in response, I stuttered and stumbled, stammering my greetings, but from start to finish never mentioned Qiuzi. I lacked the courage to say to him, *Your Qiuzi, our Qiuzi, is gone.*

After five days of torment, I took the same night train home. Standing at the door and ringing the bell, I waited, hoping against hope for a miracle, feeling as if a whole lifetime had gone by. I stood there a long while to give her enough time, imagining her getting dressed as she walked to the door after coming out of the bathroom or having just woken up in the bedroom. In the end, I took out my key, finally convinced that darkness remained and that there was no one left in the world to turn on a light for me. I wanted to cry, but could no longer weep properly. The silent darkness, quiet and yet roaring like tidal water, was about to inundate me.

My life became increasingly bleak. Each day passed both quickly and slowly. Fast like a nightmare that vanishes the moment you wake up; slow as if in a deathly trance. I forced myself to focus on work, since the construction project was unstoppable. The rains could come at any time and would create oceans of muddy water, overburdening the drainage system and flooding the newly landscaped hillside.

Summer was nearly over when the Motor clan came together for an al fresco banquet in the shade of the trees. The adults sat at one table, while the children ran around catching the cicadas that chirped mournfully all over the mountain, but went quiet when they were put into glass jars. Acting as the host, Boss Motor made sure the food was served at the right intervals and personally distributed large skewers of meat to each of his brothers, affectionately calling out their names, as if they were long separated family members coming together from far-flung corners.

I was in charge of serving the spirits. Lively conversations were struck up after they downed their first glass.

'I hear the impact of SARS was as serious as the big earthquake. Lots of construction sites in the city had to shut down.'

'Sure, people are scared. I haven't heard of anyone going out to sign a contract wearing a surgical mask.'

'So should we wait a while or follow our original schedule?'

'Nothing will happen on this plot of land if we fail again.'

'Tell us, Number Eight, how could something like this have happened? We suffer a natural disaster every time you take over a project.'

Boss Motor poured himself another drink and drained it. He smacked his lips and then bit down on the lower one, his pupils dilating as he stared at the rim of his glass. I easily read this expression of his, knowing that anger was boiling up inside; but he managed to suppress his rage. By the time his lips relaxed, the lower one had turned white, an obvious sign of his silent struggle. Evidently, he realized that getting close to his brothers was more difficult than catching a bird in flight, and breaking up a rare family reunion so quickly would be unwise.

He wore a melancholy look when he told me to go with him out beyond the trees, where he unzipped his trousers and faced the distant mountain. 'Keep an eye on the temple overseer,' he said with a snort. 'That chap's patience is thin as paper. I heard he's been talking about selling the land again. We'll be toast if the others fall in line. Go and chat him up to see what he's got in mind. I didn't cause SARS. Why doesn't he just sell the temple? A lousy temple overseer who mouths Buddhist prayers all day long, he's obsessed with money. He's got to know that we'd get a shitty price if we sold the land in the middle of a panic.'

'Let me think about it. I really don't know what to say to him.'

'You made the proposal, so go and convince him with your ideas. Or tell him to go fishing in the ocean. Maybe the fucker could catch a marlin. In my view, he's worse than a leaky boat.' He zipped up and, seeing my listless look, added, 'We can't rush things now, so take a few days' leave and go down there. Calling her every day doesn't do a damn bit of good. Keep looking for her, since you don't want to file a missing persons report. Take my car and go and find her, even if you have to drive all the way to Africa.'

The al fresco banquet continued. He told a joke when he returned to his seat, amusing his sisters-in-law, all those good ladies, so much that they giggled and shrieked.

I didn't waste a second. Driving off in Boss Motor's SUV, I relied upon my imagination to come up with a search plan. I'd start at the northern coast, going as far as Jinguashi. I imagined Qiuzi hiding in some distant corner on the coast, where each and every day she gazed over at the mountain where I was. Following the coastline, I tracked the sound of waves, constantly recalling how she cradled her camera, sitting behind me on my scooter. She was looking through her viewfinder before we'd even reached the beach. I never did take her to a real sand-covered beach back then; all we saw was a man-made breakwater, and she managed only to capture an evening glow, never the sunset she wanted.

I couldn't find a single reason to hate her.

Not until I reached the eastern coast did I realize that no one could really take shelter in a place with billowing waves. A beach at sunset was right there in front of me, but it wasn't an image Qiuzi could see. And was an ocean still an ocean if she couldn't see it? I sped down the highway that wove round Qingshui Cliff, and had to stop several times because the steep drop disorientated me. I stumbled out of the car and squatted by the roadside to throw up. Out of despair came a decision to stay away from the coast after I reached Hualien; I would drive through inland towns instead, imagining that it was a game she and I were playing. She'd hidden away to give me a fright, and sooner or later I'd meet up with her by cruising along the streets and byways. If I slipped past and missed her she'd jump out and stop me.

'You overshot.' I heard her voice at every street corner.

It was a fruitless trip. When I got back home I realized that a whole week had passed. A letter from the bank that had stuck in the slot downstairs threw me into such confusion that I didn't open it immediately. At the kitchen table I held the envelope up to the light. It appeared to be some sort of printed matter, though it called to mind Luo Yiming, and that created waves of sharp pain. Finally I opened it, and discovered that it was an overdue payment notice for the interest.

That reminded me of a horrifying coincidence: a credit loan of three million had been approved only days before Qiuzi left home.

Her photos lay on the table, just as her treasured camera was still on the shelf. She had obviously resolved to leave them behind because of the tragic event they had led to. Was leaving them a hint for me to continue my search? I'd gone to the Luo residence three times, where I'd circled the house and waited; once I'd seen him come out with a bag of rubbish, and another time he'd been locking up the gate and leaving after his weekend stay.

I took a closer look at the chilling photos. I hadn't had time to compliment her that night, and now it was obviously too late. In truth, she'd made incredible progress as a photographer, and I was too ignorant to detect any flaw. To be sure, there had been a secret alongside her viewfinder, another pair of eyes to help her. He had pointed at the clouds to show their proportion to the mountains and had taught her how to capture the essence of wild lilies; he had even taken special pains with the spectacular pine tree under the lone peak, squatting with his hands on his knees to whisper instructions.

I thought I'd found the place where she got out of the car that day. In the background was a relatively flat point of entry to a scenic site, where a road sign was partially visible through the treetops. I ran out and bought a magnifying glass; the shaky script finally mustered the courage to tell me its name: Ta ta ka.

12

A fog settled in around three in the afternoon after I'd climbed my way to Tataka. A drizzle that had set in on the road up had driven off even those tourists who had come with umbrellas. Evidently, Qiuzi had reached the mountain saddle before noon, the only time when the sun was bright and clear enough for her to snap photos of the mountain range.

What had she done after the fog arrived? She would have had no reason to linger, so could someone have asked her to stay? Or maybe they could have gone down the mountain and driven through Dongpu, as it was on the way to Shuili – as I discovered when I drove through to get a feel for the road. Down there people were waving at passing cars to drum up business for the many B&Bs scattered among the charming country roads. He must have veered into a path leading to a hot springs and removed the car key, making her lose her bearings and sink into a fog so dense she couldn't find her way home.

During the year following that trip to Tataka, I pretty much travelled every road, all but the bleak path to death.

I even tried travelling that latter path many times. During

a noontime break at the site, I took a machete to clear away the underbrush and dropped down to the hillside stream behind the temporary clubhouse, and from there climbed to the water's source, where I flung myself into the upstream waterfall. Then I floated downstream like a corpse to a deep pool. But dying was hard, probably because it wasn't my time. I was often caught between rocks in the stream and failed to drift along in the current like a fallen leaf or a dog drowning in a bottomless pool. I continued my attempt in the rapids, pretending to be new at swimming and diving under, flailing my arms and kicking my feet to sink to the bottom, so I could experience a true death.

Unfortunately, I always struggled to the surface just as I was about to succeed. In addition to swallowing too much water, I was also violently shoved away by a mysterious, dark force. It was then that I saw him. He suddenly emerged in the rippling water, as if his dead soul had taken over every waterway, his ghostly pale, bloated face exposed as usual, his eyes, pecked by fish, snapping open at me.

My body, a shell back from death, continued to live in an eternal dark night, like the walking dead.

The Angel of Death refused to grant me my wish to die, and my boss wouldn't let me quit. Seasons came and went, but I remained in the grip of painful sorrow, as though paralyzed.

On the hill flowers bloomed even more brilliantly each season, despite the continuing market slump. Work on the property slowly came to a halt, and the machinery was taken away. For two years, members of the Motor clan came up for hikes during their New Year reunions, and to see if Brother Number Eight had been doing a good job at maintaining the ancestral land. No one but Boss Motor mentioned 'The Old

Man and the Sea' again. I too wished the old man would never return. If struggling means bringing a tragedy to its conclusion, or if one can experience rebirth only after a tragedy has ended, then where was I at that moment? Was my tragedy just beginning, not yet even at midpoint? Would I have the ability to stay the course? If I never heard from her again, what could a rebirth without Qiuzi symbolize?

Heaven had played a joke on me that winter. The symbolism was clear.

It had happened one evening.

I'd hitched a ride with Boss Motor to the foothills so I could catch the bus home for some winter clothes. He was in a hurry to attend a dinner, so he left after giving me instructions. A taxi pulled up before the bus arrived, and out popped two young men who asked me if I needed a ride; then they dragged me into the back seat before I could even respond.

They stuck pistols under my arm and in my gut. I couldn't see their faces, but their gruff, threatening voices came through loud and clear. 'You've got the wrong man,' I said.

A pistol slammed against my ribs.

'Don't talk unless we tell you to,' the bigger, tougher one said.

They emptied my pockets, and the short bloke snorted when he checked my wallet.

'Should we burn him, like the last one?' the driver turned to ask.

'Let's give him a chance,' his huskier partner said in a hushed voice. 'Where were you going?'

A fist landed, knocking the wind out of me before I managed an answer.

'You don't even have an ATM card. What are we going to

do with you? Think fast and come up with someone in Taipei who can save you. Tell them you've been kidnapped by three men, and that if they're a true friend they'll bring ransom money.'

'Or you can phone home and tell them to find the money.'

'Don't tell us you don't even have a wife.'

They took turns talking, so I chose to remain silent, only to end up with more punches. An uppercut sent my tooth through my lip, and a hand pushed my face down to my knees. It abruptly went quiet in the car before they began a whispered discussion in underworld jargon. 'We don't grab just anyone,' the tough guy said. 'We know what we're looking for, and we'll knock off any chicken-shit who wets himself. But you, buddy, you're different. It's your bad luck you got out of a Mercedes. That marked you for us. You won't do yourself any favours if you tell us you don't have any money. We've got all night.'

My mouth was pressed shut against my knees, so I couldn't have replied even if I'd wanted to. Blood that had filled the cracks between my teeth was slowly drying, but another elbow jab provided a fresh supply.

The taxi proceeded at an even speed as we drove into the night; I could sense that they were circling a large area.

What was happening presaged a future I was unable to anticipate; my shoes were black, the same as the mat under them. I had no idea why it had to be me, but didn't know why it shouldn't be either. To keep from suffocating, I furtively forced open a corner of my mouth, and each time I breathed, my knees felt sticky from the moist hot air. It must have been quite late by then, but dawn was still far away. All I'd wanted was to go home for some warm clothes.

With difficulty I arched my back and stretched my lips wide enough to say, 'Take me home.'

That was met with guffaws from all three men. Their laughter stopped abruptly, ending on an eerie, grim note.

The short one to my right finally said, 'I think we can give it a try.'

'What do you mean?'

'He looks clear-headed enough to mean what he says. I don't think he's lying.'

'Well then, stop roughing him up. Give him some water and find out where he lives.'

I gave them the address, likely more than a hundred kilometres away, but that didn't bother them. The taxi turned and sped off. The driver tuned into a traffic channel. There was a minor prang around Xinzhu, but the police were on site.

'What do you have at home?' the short one asked.

'There should be some money in the drawer, and a camera.'

'And your wife really isn't home?'

'Tell him we'll kill anyone we see, Number Three. No more questions. I want to get some sleep.'

The taxi arrived in Taichung.

They told the short bloke to go with me. The wall clock said 3.05 when we walked in. I went to wash my face, a pistol pressed into my back the whole time; Qiuzi's camera was already hanging from his shoulder.

'On one job we didn't get any money, and Number One tied me inside a hemp sack and starved me for five days. So tell me why you only have five thousand in the drawer and make it quick, or I'll be in big trouble.'

He continued his search, eventually digging out a deposit book and a carved signature seal, both news to me. Before we left, while taking the camera off his shoulder and dropping it onto the table, he told me to change into cloth shoes. 'Walk softly or I'll let you have it. I've got your deposit book, so you can keep the camera. Number One hates things like that. They produce evidence.'

'Can I ask you for a favour?' I said.

'Don't worry, we'll let you go. Number One never lies.'

'You don't have to go through the trouble. I'll turn around and you shoot me in the back.'

He was stunned and averted his eyes. 'I can't make that kind of decision.'

Number One glanced at the figure in the deposit book when we got back to the taxi. 'See, you said we nabbed the wrong guy, but we didn't. With three million, you're our god of fortune. Get some sleep now, and we'll keep quiet. The bank opens at nine a.m. You'll go in at 9.10. Number Three, you'll go with him again. I'm glad you're getting better at this.'

Shorty started to snore soon after poking a straw into a soft drink and stuffing the other end into my mouth. Number One's head sagged as he too fell asleep. The car glided under the shade of some trees, where the driver took over guarding me. After turning off the engine, he rested his elbow on the dashboard to point his gun at me.

We were right on time. When we finally walked up the steps to the bank, Shorty stuck his pistol, which was concealed under his jacket, into my side, while the other two kept watch from the car window, weapons in hand. The teller took my deposit book and seal for verification when we were at the counter; in the meantime, someone stood up from the manager's desk at the far wall.

Ah, we meet again . . .

He stood by the sofa reserved for clients and invited me over. I quickly staggered forward but had to slow down when Shorty jammed his pistol hard into my ribs. Guided by his concealed weapon, I inched along.

It had been a long time since I'd last seen him. Luo Yiming, who had been so thoughtful, still wore a simple, kind expression, one that matched his white shirt and blue tie, all adding to the air of an immaculate gentleman. In contrast, I stood before him looking worn out, after a sleepless night; my collar was stained with blood, my light jacket was rumpled after my prolonged confinement, my black trousers were oddly paired with white cloth shoes, I was unshaven, and my gaze lacked focus.

Of course he'd noted my bizarre appearance, as his face froze. He must have been puzzled, but he quickly regained his composure. I thought he was able to remain calm because he was planning to signal with his eyes to the nearby security guard, who would get the message. Or he'd say something to Shorty, and then he would know something was wrong the minute he opened his mouth to respond, and that would buy some time to rescue me.

But, as it turned out, he decided to do neither, even though he had sensed something. I watched him sit down almost regally and then lean against the back of his chair. Suddenly looking completely relaxed, he casually offered me a cup of tea and stroked his chin. When the clerk brought over bundles of cash, it was time to see me off. After a cool glance my way, he stood up.

13

They fled south after getting what they wanted and dumped me in a deserted graveyard.

I was in the middle of a bamboo grove that connected the criss-crossing rows of tombs. I stumbled and rolled down the slope all the way to an industrial road, where I crawled over to a telegraph pole, planning to flag down a passing car. But the only thing that came my way were ice-cold gusts of wind. My cries for help sounded shrill, unlike those of a normal human being, as if joined by Qiuzi's shouts, two people calling out together to anyone but Luo Yiming.

I'll never forget the look he gave me, a man I'd respected. He had forsaken me at a critical moment. So he really was guilty; no wonder, then, that he had not wanted me to live.

But live I must.

Night had all but fallen by the time I rushed back to the mountain, where I gave a pathetic excuse for having taken a day off – I said I'd accidently left a bag on the train. Qiuzi had been defiled; that was the only thing that was real to me. Luo Yiming had confessed as much, with his indifference. The whereabouts of the three thugs didn't concern me; all I wanted was to talk to someone, tell him I'd returned, that not only was I over my desire to die, but I had also made it through a particularly dark and painful stage of my life.

I wanted to stand on my own two feet again, yet I found myself missing a certain innate ability – I had always previously been able to conjure up Qiuzi's face whenever I thought of her, but now it took great effort to form an image by pulling together memories associated with her, starting with her name, and then her dimple, followed by our entangled bodies in bed, and the hidden scar on the side of her breast...

I remembered parts of her, but not her.

In my attempt to see her clearly, I slowly lost the ability to talk to people, for I was distracted much of the time, as if keeping watch on a door in my mind, afraid of missing her when she eventually walked in through it, or of waiting in vain when it was impossible that she would ever enter.

Boss Motor told me not to feel bad when he realized what was bugging me, saying that it was natural. *Will you still remember the bath suite in an old house after you move into a new one?*

I thought of carrying her photo with me so that I could take it out any time I wanted to recall her image; but if someone you love lies only in your pocket, doesn't that mean you've lost her?

Life had gone on like that until last winter. Working late into the night each day, I edited and finalized the delayed proposal, with additional notes on a preliminary study of ecological rehabilitation as well as a comprehensive analysis of market trends after the SARS outbreak. Then I chose the afternoon of our year-end meeting, when suddenly I felt restless, to ask a favour of Boss Motor as I handed him my report.

I said, 'Do you remember the time we were at the appliance store, and there was a club upstairs . . .'

'Of course I remember. My only regret is that I can't remember every woman there.'

'Can we have dinner and then you take me there to check it out?'

'You should've mentioned this earlier. Sooner or later every man will regret not doing something he should have done.'

'I just felt it was time. Tonight should be the night.'

It was still early when we got to the club, so there weren't many clients there yet. But some of the women were already waiting in the transparent booths. One was listlessly fiddling with her hair, another was blowing on her newly polished nails, and one had cocked her head to watch the eaves outside, like a pigeon. But not the one I was looking for. Using gestures, I described her height, her pale, thin face, and the way she pulled her long hair behind her right shoulder. 'I know who you mean,' the waiter said softly. 'No one ever asked for her, so she hasn't been here for a long time.

'Listen to me,' he added. 'See that girl in a black trench coat? She's not bad. The one who's standing up. Yes, that one. If you can't decide, step over to the top of the stairs and I'll send her out. She'll open her coat for you to see that she won't be wearing anything underneath.'

'I'm not here to do that.'

'Then what – you're here to meet your future wife?'

I must have offended him, for his tone turned cool and his patience seemed to have run out as he went and made a phone call. About half an hour later, a small door at the rear of the lobby opened quietly, and there she was. Dressed plainly, obviously because of the unexpected nature of the phone call, she'd draped her hair over her right shoulder and was hesitant; she looked shyly in the direction pointed by the waiter, seemingly eager to know who might have asked for her. Clearly, she hadn't had a client for a long time.

'She'll cost you,' the waiter said as he anxiously whispered an amount in my ear. I had to whisper back, 'I won't mind, even if I have to eat steamed buns for three meals a day starting next month.' That helped defrost his attitude, as an understanding sorrow flashed in his eyes. He turned and told her to get her bag and go with me.

We walked out of the club and onto a side street, her in front. Her feet were kept busy hopping to avoiding rain puddles, so I had to stop frequently to wait for her. I probably should have taken her hand, but I abandoned the idea for fear that she might somehow consider that dirty. I'd also thought of asking her name, but gave that up too. She had smiled at me before we left, and I hadn't expected to see her face harden once we were out on the street; it was as if she had a strict rule about the transaction – she was selling her flesh, but not her feelings. No wonder she was quiet the whole time.

She had it all wrong, of course. I just wanted to find a coffee shop where she could sit across from me for a couple of hours; that would be enough for me. Everyone has a doppelgänger, and since Qiuzi wasn't around, I'd had to pay for a copy. She'd looked so much like Qiuzi at first, but now, after pulling a long face the whole time, her smile perfunctory and insincere, as though wearing a mask, the similarities began to fade.

For my part, I wondered why it had suddenly started raining. Rain permeated the memories I shared with Qiuzi; in fact, it had always come at the most significant moments in our life. So this woman, who was really Qiuzi's double, had even brought rain into our encounter. In that case, how much more of Qiuzi would be duplicated on her body? I found myself secretly looking forward to finding out.

With her skinny figure and cheap clothes, she certainly was overpriced when viewed from behind. Her handbag was obviously from a street vendor, and the boots were worth little, especially now that they were waterlogged. But when I followed her to the hotel entrance, I felt an unwarranted happiness rising inside. Yes, not going to a coffee shop had probably been a good idea; in addition to her face, I might find more of Qiuzi on her body. How could she be overpriced then? If she only had a passing resemblance, it would have been worth it.

14

If it had been my boss and not me, he would likely have taken a shower right after walking into the room. He would have turned the hot tap all the way up and, as the water crashed down, sung at the top of his voice Pavarotti's lines in 'We Are the World' before coming out stark naked to push the woman down on the bed like catching a little bird.

It was my first time in such a room.

To hide the fact that I was new to this, I put her hand on my knee and gave it a gentle caress. She had long, smooth fingers on fair hands below her sleeve; I felt an urge to unbutton it.

Unhappy with that, she pulled her hand back and took off her boots instead. Then she turned around to take off her short jacket. If I didn't stop her, she'd be standing there naked before I was ready. This really wasn't what I had in mind.

So I had to say, 'If you don't mind, let's turn off the lights to have the room in total darkness.'

'You're not doing that to scare me, are you?'

'No, that's not it. I just thought it could be fun.'

She looked at me, scrutinized me, actually, surprised and yet pleased. As if afraid that I might change my mind, she nodded emphatically, a cheerful glint in her eyes. *Now?* she asked as she got up and walked to the switch by the door, where she turned and looked at me again, this time with an impish grin. The lights went out one by one in sequence with her footsteps. I turned off the last one, a desk lamp, when she reached the chair beside me. At that instant we disappeared into the darkness.

'Can I turn on a light to take a shower?' she asked softly.

I nodded, but then realized that we couldn't see each other, so I muttered my consent.

She began to grope her way around; after scooping her handbag up from the chair, she stood up and slowly moved past my knees, her fingers touching the sheet lightly. When she finally made it to the door, she turned on the bathroom light.

'Why do you want to do it this way? It wastes a lot of time.'

She slipped inside before I could respond, and the room returned to darkness. I could hear spray from the showerhead hit the glass door, like water running through a neighbour's pipes late at night.

Amid the faint intermittent sound of running water, she began to hum a lively tune, smoothly but for the last few notes, which rose and fell like bursting bubbles. As I recalled her earlier cold look, I wondered why she now felt like singing. What could have inspired her to do that? Maybe she just found it amusing to have all the lights turned off.

It would soon be New Year, so there was still street noise at this late hour. A pedlar selling roasted sweet potatoes passed by, followed by a van from which clothing was being hawked by someone with a hoarse voice. I could hear movement in the room, as she quietly opened the bathroom door and headed my way, her feet clad in paper slippers, like the splash of oars from a slow boat. She muttered something coquettish, but with a hint of childish naughtiness, as if playing hide and seek. Finally, when her hand found my thigh, she leaned against me, sounding relieved.

With her sitting across my thighs, I sensed her naked body under the thin bathrobe, like an aroma drifting from a little steamer whose lid has just been removed. She took my hand and put it inside the robe. There was still dampness under her breast, moist and smooth to the touch, and I felt myself drifting off course in the dark. No longer shy, I held her tightly and even began to explore with my hands before burying my face between her breasts. She was not Qiuzi, but close enough for me.

'Your turn,' she said.

The tone of her brief utterance sounded astonishingly like Qiuzi. I put my hands around her neck to pull her into my arms, but I ended up frightening her. Trying to get away, she tilted her head as far back as she could to keep my hand from reaching into her long hair.

My hand shrank back as if struck by an electric shock, but it was too late.

One side of her skull was flattened, like a broken rock hidden in trees.

I jerked my hand away, but my head remained between her breasts. The surrounding darkness suddenly became irritating, and I was immobilized by a sense of numbness. At a loss for words, I could feel only my heart beating wildly between our two bodies.

'It's so rare that you wanted the lights off. I thought I might stand a chance of measuring up tonight.' She laughed sadly. 'Obviously it didn't work. I should go now.'

How long had it taken her to grow her hair long enough to cover up such a wretched shadow?

Instead of responding, I began to cry into the dark.

IV

*An enemy destroyed in a dream; a cherry tree
blooming at the head of the bed*

We don't have to start if you're not ready, Miss Baixiu said.

She was still waiting for my reply, leaning forward and stopping me in mid-breath. I tilted back, suddenly awakened to a suspicion that I was under her control. With the trace of an enigmatic smile, she placed her hands in the centre of the old-fashioned indigo cloth, now and then smoothing the creased edges while she waited, before bringing her hands back in front of her and clasping them together as though offering a New Year greeting.

'What's there to get ready for? You can start now,' I said.

'Your mind is elsewhere, it's a mass of jumbled thoughts.'

Shall we start? She'd grown tired of waiting. She brought a basket out from under the table, removed its woven bamboo lid, and took out more than a dozen jars and bottles of various shapes and styles, which she then arranged in the space between her arms. The odd porcelain pieces came in a variety of colours. To be honest, they were actually quite tasteful. After she had meticulously arranged them, she held her palms together and said, 'I'll try not to embarrass myself.'

She placed a candleholder on the table, and then added a small piece of charcoal on top and lit it.

Once the charcoal was burning red, she picked it up with a pair of silver tongs and buried it in the ashes of a small incense burner.

'Everyone suffers from an unspeakable pain, like this fire hidden in the ashes,' she said as she took out a feather, metallic blue in colour, with lovely purple edges.

Turning the feather into what she called an incense brush, she swept the white ash in the incense burner into a tiny mound in the centre, and then combed it into horizontal lines to give it the appearance of slim rivulets in a parched landscape.

She then brought out a small silver disk, saying it was mica, and placed it directly above the buried charcoal, after which she poured in a pinch of dark brown powder from one of the bottles. A hidden volcano began to smoulder silently.

'Make a wish,' Miss Baixiu said. 'What would you like?'

1

What else could I wish for? Let me think.

The reeds have all turned white beyond the window. If there's anything I could ask for, I'd like everyone to go away. I don't want anyone else to be here when I see Qiuzi again, since I have long been the only one who has been saddened by her disappearance.

That's the only thing I want now, because she's about to show up.

She could be hiding amid the waves of reeds, where she has lingered until she has spotted a light on in the shop. A look of pleasant surprise will illuminate her face. 'I didn't see this last year.' That's right. How could this have been here last year, such a cheerless time? The gravel path to the door was hastily laid. Even the sad moon was nowhere in sight, let alone lamplight.

She's been gone four years. Can a woman wander through life that long? I've spent every New Year's Eve at her parents' house. Her mother always looks up at the hillside with tears in her eyes, and an expectant look greets the sound of every approaching car. An inquisitive wall clock is ticking away in a corner, and none of us has an answer as we sit around the table at a silent New Year's Eve dinner. It's the same every year; we don't even set off firecrackers.

How can Miss Baixiu revive such an ignoble soul? In the face of self-reproach, searching and helpless panic, I managed to survive on the courage provoked by her father's pitiless behaviour. But it was a woman, one who was unknown to all, who prompted me to give up everything and come here.

I burst out crying in that dark room, Miss Baixiu. Do you believe me?

The woman was frightened when she heard me crying. 'Please stop. You're disappointed in me, aren't you?'

I couldn't see the dejected look on her face, but I knew I'd behaved badly. I dried my tears on my sleeve, still unsure what to do next. It would make her feel even worse if I got up and walked out, so I kept my arms around her; her body had cooled following my crying fit.

'Don't worry about me. We don't have to do it if you don't feel like it,' she said.

Instead of letting her go, I shook my head, wanting her to stay.

'Do you really want me to? I nearly crushed you.'

I worked up enough passion to put my lips on hers. She stopped struggling and asked out of the corner of her mouth, 'Why were you crying? You sounded so sad.' Before she could finish, I looped my arms back around her neck, conscious of the illusion of Qiuzi that had been released from her breasts. More at ease now, she reached up to smooth my hair as she told me she'd sustained the injury to her skull in a traffic accident; her boyfriend left her after that, and her mother was all she had now.

'What about you?' she asked.

'Me? I'd rather not go there; you don't want to know.'

As well as the resemblance in the shape of her face and her features, Qiuzi had also been in an astonishingly similar predicament; she must have experienced such a penetrating heartache that she'd decided to leave me, taking her misfortune with her on that early morning before the first ray of daylight.

We spent a long time in that darkened room until the front desk called and asked us to check out, thus tactfully lowering the curtain on our film while it was still dark. When the lights came back on, I had to squint, and as my eyes adjusted to the brightness, I watched her walk to the foot of the bed to pick up her strewn clothes. She started to put on her knickers, but then she turned around, topless, as if the room were still submerged in darkness. In no hurry to put her bra back on, she went over to the window and pulled the curtains apart to look into the night sky.

'Let me buy you dinner. It's not often I earn clean money like this.'

As I stood on a street corner and watched her walk off, I realized I hadn't contacted Boss Motor. When I finally did, I was surprised to learn that he had checked out of his room a while before and was singing and drinking with friends at their guest house on Jilin Road. I heard the tumult in the background as he shouted into the phone:

'How did it go? Had a great time, I guess.'

I summoned the courage to tell him I'd like a year-long leave of absence after the New Year. If the company couldn't make an exception, I'd simply hand in my notice. He was shouting and yelling into the phone, but someone next to him was singing a Taiwanese song which merged with the sound of a train whistle in the music video, quickly drowning out his voice.

It was early summer when I first showed up here two months after that. The cicadas were chirping more loudly on the far side of the stream than on my side. The abandoned, squat house had nothing left but an electricity meter. It now belonged to the original owner's son, who probably mistook me for a famous artist and as a result charged me so little rent it was like free lodging. He came every day to help me clear the area and even asked his carpenter uncle to built a loft for me.

On the day the coffee shop opened for business, my only customer was a passing sausage vendor whose cartwheels rattled over the gravel path, making his uncooked sausage sway violently on the rack. He said he'd just shut up shop at the temple, and the unexpected appearance of lights here had piqued his curiosity. He'd thought he was finally going to meet some ghosts. His stove was still warm, so he fanned the fire and roasted some sausages by the side of the road. Hatred still simmering inside me, I wanted to ask him about Luo Yiming, but, afraid that he might make my arrival public knowledge, I stifled my unuttered question, swallowing it along with two of his sausages.

From the day I had vowed to remain silent up to now, I'd managed to keep my mouth sealed and not breathe a word; the name Luo Yiming would have ceased to exist for me if Miss Baixiu had not kept coming with her threats and promises, and if her father had not showed up for that cup of coffee.

What I wanted was to find Qiuzi, her and her purity.

Nothing else mattered to me any more.

So, frankly, it was comical and confusing when Miss Baixiu, in all seriousness, asked me to make a wish. But I followed her example and shut my eyes to satisfy her fantasy that she was a teacher for my soul.

Finally she started tinkering.

First she demonstrated the required speed of inhaling and exhaling, the pace of holding the incense burner, and how one sniffed the incense. Once she finished the cycle, she wanted me to repeat what I'd just learned, so I picked up the burner. Like an idiot who has stumbled through a genie's door, I didn't dare ask any questions or say anything, fearful that my laughter would send the ashes I was holding flying.

She used four different kinds of incense, saying they embodied the essence of the four seasons. Once we had inhaled a scent three times, she replaced it with another. This was when she spoke, in a slightly hoarse voice. Like someone who had returned to the mundane world after her spirit had travelled to an ethereal realm, she was curious to know how I, an ordinary person, felt. She asked a string of questions: *what did you smell? What were you thinking? Did you see a sea of clouds? Or did you walk through a forest? Did you feel your body and mind relax? No? Not yet? Really?*

To help her accomplish her noble mission, I resorted to nodding repeatedly and making up something about seeing a sea of clouds when I spotted a Boeing aeroplane flying past, trailed by a wavy feather that was a soft black, which I thought should be me, reflecting the golden rays in the sky . . .

'That's ridiculous. There couldn't be a Boeing.'

'Okay, it was a reconnaissance plane trying to rescue my soul, just like you are.'

I tried not to laugh at her and her magic formula. Honestly, she'd done everything she could to save her father or salvage my conscience; she'd taken it all so seriously, bringing with her a whole set of props she'd gathered just for this trip. *You've put a lot into this, Miss Baixiu.*

2

A rare visitor showed up a few days after that.

A black car with tinted windows parked on the dirt road beyond the gravel path and blasted its horn into the shop. The driver's door opened and out stepped Old Guo. He waved at me to come over. Then the back window slowly rolled down to reveal a pair of oversized sunglasses, an attempt to give me a scare. Finally, he spoke up: 'You should have come out to greet me. I made this trip specially to see you.'

Boss Motor was now a somewhat different man; gone were the betel nuts and the heavy smell of alcohol. He walked fairly nimbly on feet clad in regular leather shoes. Nothing wrong with his feet, it seemed. I led him over to a window seat, where the incense still lingered from Miss Baixiu's visit. He sniffed the air and asked what essential oils I was spraying, adding that he could smell the tiniest dust mote since he quit smoking.

'How are you doing? I've been counting the days till this place closes.'

'Not yet. My year's leave won't be up until the spring.'

'I'll bet you'll still be selling coffee here all alone even if you take a hundred years' leave.'

He looked around before sticking his head out the window and calling to Old Guo to come in. Then he fixed his gaze on the loft, like the rookie policeman had done. 'Stop being such a fool.' He turned back to look at me. 'She won't come.'

'She will if she remembers.'

'I see. It's like a scene from a film. How long are you going to wait? Waiting isn't going to bring her back.'

He cocked his head to look at the embankment outside. 'I've thought about bringing my wife back too. I heard that some bloke barged into the restaurant and knocked her out. She told her employees not to tell me. How terrible is that? Most likely, it wasn't because she didn't want me to feel bad, it was because she was afraid I *wouldn't* feel bad.'

I made him an old-fashioned Mandheling coffee. His loyalty to a cup of coffee illustrated the limited extent of his devotion to all things, as far as I could recall, so I was surprised to detect a fleeting wistfulness when he spoke of his wife.

Old Guo asked for a cup of black tea. An early-winter wind swept fallen leaves under the car beneath the four o'clock sky. I joined Boss Motor in a cup as he updated me on the progress in the mountain over the past six months. 'The workers spotted a couple of muntjacs a few days ago. They had sneaked over from the stream for the fruit. I was told they looked like a doe and her fawn, so obviously our ecological rehabilitation is getting better all the time. But we had a thief too, one with lousy luck. He must have been greatly disappointed in your old room. He took a dump in there.'

'What about your brothers?'

'I knew you'd ask about them. You know more about our

complicated relationship than anyone, which is the real reason for my visit today. You know, all seven of them have been very nice to me lately, even stopped calling me Number Eight. They're fully aware that I spend all my time there for their sake. The landscaping has really taken off. Even a recently trans-planted old Bishop wood decided to come back from the dead when it saw all the vibrant vegetation around it. You know what I'm saying, don't you, buddy? It's about time, and I'm still waiting for you to return to get started on the final stages of the pre-sale. You need to pull yourself together.'

I went over to make him another cup. As I waited for the coffee mill to grind the beans, I noticed the tail end of that familiar car peeking out from amid the trees. She'll have to wait a long time, I said to myself. Boss Motor asked about Qiuzi in a voice so soft it put his driver to sleep. 'You told me you had no family when you came for the interview. I was startled by your pitiful appearance mainly because my biggest problem at the time was having too big a family.'

I smiled foolishly. I had indeed looked pitiful.

'You pulled a fast one on me. What you said that day was pretty silly, but super-impressive.'

Who could remember that? I gave him a surprised look.

'You said you needed to accomplish something before you could have her.'

He stopped me as I was about to refill Guo's cup, and that pause seemed to make my heart clench up. I really had said something like that.

'So what have you accomplished? Think about it. You wear a hangdog expression all day long, and she wouldn't dare return even if she wanted to, since she'd surely blame herself for your misery. You need to find a way to cheer up. I learned that after countless bouts of torment inflicted on me by the other seven.'

It was getting dark outside, but he changed his mind about leaving right away. Instead he told Guo to bring the car over. 'We haven't shared a drink for a long time now. I hear there's a stand around here that sells delicious stewed pork cheeks. Let's talk over dinner, what do you say? We'll go over the pre-sale promotion again. There's been an upturn in the property market lately. We'll probably have to revise our pricing structure upward, at least a little, but most importantly, we won't touch your proposal. Everyone's watching wide-eyed to see how well you do. The Old Man and the Sea. It's not every day that the fighting spirit in life can be adapted to the construction business. It's truly groundbreaking. Do what you have to do. Cheer up, so you won't look worse than an old man.'

The car was still there when we got ready to leave. I hesitated as I was pulling down the rolling door and, suddenly feeling bad for her, decided to leave it up and left the glass door unlocked.

It was even darker when Boss Motor's car pulled off onto the street. After driving around for a while, he made a couple of phone calls to get the address for the pork cheek stand. In the past he'd have gone to the first stand he saw.

'You live such an isolated life, I'll bet you don't even know where to buy pork, let alone pork cheeks.'

We stopped in an alley behind the Mazu temple. Instead of ordering beer, he told Guo to fetch a bottle of super fine sorghum spirits from the boot of his car. He started talking after downing two cups, but only about what he'd been doing to improve his health. He and a few friends were now into saxophones and had been taking regular lessons.

'The instructor said I have the lung capacity of a frog. Shit. I practise and practise until my sides hurt even when I sneeze. But I think my dead diaphragm is coming back alive, and when I play I sound like I'm having a fight.'

I was reminded of the summer night when we lay on the slope drinking beer. He'd been talking about Pavarotti's High C and his worries that the world's best tenor wouldn't make it each time he performed. Boss Motor had actually been talking about himself. But now he'd changed. He had previously needed three cars to build up his confidence when he left his house; he didn't need that any longer. A saxophone was enough to earn him bragging rights.

I was a little drunk when I returned to the shop. Miss Baixiu had left in her car.

But she'd been inside and there was an envelope on the counter. It didn't contain a note; instead there were two photos. One, a familiar scene, was of the large cherry tree at their house; the other rendered me speechless.

3

Miss Baixiu, who had missed seeing me earlier, called before I had even sobered up; she was eager and anxious, like someone looking for a lost item. She said that seasonal changes had forced them to increase the dosage of her father's medicine. She'd had to wait to call until he finally fell asleep. *How long have you been back? Were you drunk? Whose car was that?* She couldn't get over the fact that I had been taken away, just like that.

'I thought those two thugs had kidnapped you.'

'Were those two pictures taken outside your house?'

'Yes. It's the same house, the one you know. My father took the one with the cherry blossoms last year. He took a few of them each March as keepsakes.'

'I want to know about the other one.'

'The cherry tree's gone, that's all.'

'Why?'

'I thought I'd walked up to the wrong house the last time I came home. The ground was cleared for a large patch of fuchsia. He was very proud of it, saying the garden looked bigger, and he could see blooming flowers every day. A gardener told me that when he dug down he'd found that the cherry tree's smaller roots were all rotten. He thought the tree had been fed with salt water for a very long time.'

'That picture you left really hit me hard.'

She said nothing for a moment, and I could tell that she was choking up when she spoke again. 'These two pictures more or less replicate my father's life, with cherry blossoms and then without. I suppose life is pretty much like that. I left them for you as a contrast, not to gain your sympathy.'

When she recovered, she said that the month before she'd declined an invitation to participate in a joint photography exhibit.

'That's why I was so eager to see you. He can't give up the exhibit now that he no longer has his pride and joy, the cherry tree. So I turned in a late consent form, and now I'm selecting photos for the exhibit. It occurred to me that it would be profoundly meaningful if you took part in the process, giving each photo a caption. It could be the best medicine for him.'

Of course it would be profoundly meaningful, I said silently as I hung up.

In the photo, the Luo garden looked bare. All that remained were black tiles and white walls, which had before been shrouded by the crown of the cherry tree; this seemed to be a test of my memory. It had been dazzlingly red when Qiuzi had pushed the shutter on her camera for the first time in her life. The cherry blossoms brilliantly tinted her smiling face. I still remembered how she'd taken the picture from inside the garden, thus cropping off many old branches that had reached over the wall.

Luo Yiming must have been clear-headed when he poured

salt water onto the roots. The cherry tree had not caused his illness, but it might as well have, since, a dangerous kind of beauty, its blooming had led to the decline of everything. He knew better than anyone that he had pushed himself into an abyss under the spell of its bewitching blossoms.

In any case, there was a message of mourning in the photos; it signalled that the source of the tragedy had been terminated. Even if I were willing to write captions for the photographs, I doubt that I would have been brave enough to look at his work. Hadn't Qiuzi been led astray, following him wherever he went? She'd have held her breath, her eye behind the viewfinder, as she waited for a perfect shot framed by the master. Filled with adulation, her face brimming with my sort of naivety, she was oblivious to the notion that in his loneliness, so timeworn, he could succumb to the power of youth.

What a pity, those once brilliant blossoms, my enemy's cherry tree.

The heartache hit me after I sobered up, and the disappearance of the tree triggered even greater sorrow. Miss Baixiu's hopes would surely be dashed. How could she think that I would be high-minded enough to forgive her father, for that would amount to inserting the word 'love' into 'hate'?

I turned over the photo without the tree and wrote a brief soliloquy late that night:

An enemy destroyed in a dream; a cherry tree blooming at the head of the bed

When I finished writing I was filled with confidence that I'd now be able to put my sorrows behind me; my enemy had been destroyed without my lifting a finger, and the splendid cherry tree now bloomed for me alone. How enormously satisfying.

Yet as I climbed up to the loft and lay down, I was preoccupied with that pre-dawn morning, when Qiuzi had groped her way around in the dark. She had packed so lightly, how had she managed to get by with just a few articles of clothing? Tears welled up in my eyes at that thought, so I crawled out of the space and came down to the table, where I stared blankly at the photo. I don't know when, but at some point in my wretched state I tore it to shreds.

4

I lay in bed lethargically until noon the next day. In no mood to open for business, I decided to lock the glass door before slinking out from under the rolling shutter. The streets in town were slowly filling up with tourists, and incense was burning again at the Mazu temple after a quiet night. The food stall at the corner of the alley behind the temple was still chained and locked, so I went past it and had a simple lunch elsewhere before returning to the stall, where I managed to find the mobile phone I'd lost after a night of drinking.

The suddenly free afternoon felt too long to while away, as I couldn't stop thinking about the disappearance of the cherry tree. It was hard not to wonder if this was a subtle case of revenge; Luo Yiming might have done it intentionally to put me out of sorts and make me suffer.

I hailed a taxi and told the driver to circle the outskirts of the town, and to go slowly. He said it was hard to quote a fare unless he knew where I wanted to go, and asked if he could use the meter. 'The people in town are used to settling on a fare that's based on the distance, before we get on the road.'

I said, 'Do whatever you like, I don't care how you come up with a figure.' I wound up agreeing to use the meter, since I had no idea where I wanted to go.

'Where are you from, sir?'

'Taipei.'

'Is this your first visit?'

'First ride in a taxi.'

He slowed down as we drove by scenic spots. Filling the cab with his Haikou accent, he related ancient historical anecdotes and then moved on to the recent preservation of historical sites, unaware that his deep voice and accent were so hypnotic I nearly dozed off after we'd circled the town.

'Let's go and have a look at the beach.'

'If you want to see the ocean, we should take the outer ring road.'

'No need to do that. I just want to have a look at the ocean here.'

'Well, then, you'll see an ocean with no sandy beach.'

He turned the car round and headed straight through town. Soon I began to see traces of my former visits with Qiuzi. I asked him to stop under the rock armour at Haikou, where I forced the door open against the wind. Behind us rows of horsetail trees were bending, their leaves like messed-up hair, as the wintry coast released frenzied howls, devoid of meaning.

'I can take you to the wetland area. You'll find lots of people there. And you can take a half-day ride on a bamboo raft.'

I told him to keep driving. After passing a primary school, we drove onto an unpaved road that rose and fell. He said there was nothing more to see beyond that point, only an army barracks. So we turned and headed east towards an increasingly desolate area, where he reminded me that we were now on the road to the next town.

'This is a small place. If you're looking for someone, sir, all you have to do is give me a name.'

'What if I don't know the full name?'

'Try the surname, and I'll see. One of my fares once tested me with ten different names and ended up saying I should run for mayor.'

Luo, I said to myself.

Leaving the ring road, the cab turned around and we were back onto familiar streets and within sight of the soaring eaves of the Mazu temple. I suddenly craved a good bath as we drove by a small inn, so I asked him to go back to it and stop.

'The place where you got in at noon is just behind the inn.'

The entrance led to a hallway, at the dimly lit end of which was a hidden staircase. I saw a Taiwanese magnolia in the courtyard below when I climbed up to the second floor. The room was simple and crude, with a narrow bed against a wall, but it was a much more comfortable space than I was used to. I felt like rolling around when I threw myself on the bed, but for some reason fatigue had taken over my body, and I didn't wake up till it was dark outside.

After having managed to while away most of the day, I strolled down the street on my way back to the coffee shop. Just before I reached the gravel path, I noticed from a distance that the shop was lit up, turning the surrounding area especially dark. Staggered by what I was seeing, I took off running, and the closer I got, the more real it felt. Light from the window sifted through the bamboo beside the door.

Qiuzi. My instincts told me. Qiuzi had come and let herself in.

I was startled to see the floor littered with broken glass. That was not like Qiuzi, who would have patiently leaned against the door and looked at me, surprised and happy, as if she had been sucking on a preserved plum. I was baffled when I stuck my head in for a closer look; there next to the wall sat someone with Qiuzi's short hair, in a grey velour dress, and wearing a thin, shiny silver necklace.

I saw who it was when I walked up behind her, but that realization was immediately assailed by confusion.

Miss Baixiu could be anywhere she wanted, and this was not the time for her to make a sudden appearance. She must have come to trick me, and I fell for it. Rather than turn to look at me, she opened a lunchbox and started eating. There was another box and a pair of neatly laid-out chopsticks across from her, in front of an empty chair. It was almost seven o'clock, and she looked as though she was waiting for a tardy guest to take his seat.

'You went back to Taipei, so what are you doing here?'

'You're waiting for someone, and I'm hiding from someone.'

'Even so, you shouldn't have broken into the shop.'

'A glass door is nothing compared to a cherry tree.'

She said this unemotionally before picking up another morsel of food and eating it with a sense of purpose; she chewed slowly, the veins in her neck pulsing almost imperceptibly beneath her short hair. She turned her face away, as if she could swallow that day's dinner simply by staring at a white wall. Then she nudged the other box over and said, 'I made it myself. It's getting cold.'

The space was too cramped for me to keep standing behind her, as if we were having an argument, so I sat down and opened the box. As I ate with my head down, I sensed a pair of eyes focused on me under the short hair; when I picked up a piece of tofu skin, she seemed to be staring at it too. So I stuffed it into my mouth. I looked up, and sure enough, I saw those staring eyes no longer evasive as before, now fixed on me. She didn't stop chewing. Eating with stoic valour, she looked as if she were having a last meal before heading into battle.

This was the distance that had opened up between us by my refusal to write the captions for her.

From the darkness outside suddenly came the sound of a car door being slammed shut, followed by shouts in a man's hoarse voice. *Baixiu, Baixiu.* He kept calling, sounding like he was shouting through cupped hands. He moved from the side up to the shattered glass door, and shouted some more.

'No wonder it's so cold in here. There's nothing to stop the wind. Go and pull down the rolling door.'

'That wouldn't look good. He's here to see you, why not let him in?'

'No. He'll know what I'm thinking when you pull down the door.'

I hesitated for a long moment, but then did as she asked. I didn't see anyone out there, although the shouts didn't stop until I pulled down the door. Then a car engine roared into life. The driver had floored the gas pedal as if raging in anger. I thought he'd come crashing into the shop, and was surprised when he turned and sped down the dark road without turning on the headlights, vanishing from sight.

'You said you're hiding from someone. So that's him then.'

'A man's love can be really lousy. He came all the way to find me when I decided to end the torment, and then took off a minute later after driving two hundred kilometres to get here.'

'But at least he came.'

'He gave up as soon as he heard the door come down. I can see right through a man like that. There isn't another man like you. All you think about is Qiuzi, Qiuzi, all day long, Qiuzi.'

Miss Baixiu had broken her vow not to talk much.

Her unhappy face brightened after the car left. Putting away her lunch box before finishing what was in it, she went up to the counter to make coffee. She was clumsy but, as if celebrating something, she cried out cheerfully when she brought the coffee over, *It's hot, it's really hot*. Her slender legs were moving as if walking on clouds.

She even went over to put on some music, glided back, and stood in front of me.

'Go ahead, wait all you want,' she said in a voice tinted with bitterness, a first for her. 'I just want to tell you that if I saw Qiuzi, I'd hide her from you.'

'Why must you keep talking about her today?'

'Because I have nothing more to say. You cast my father into misery and now you've done the same to me.'

'I don't know what you mean, Miss Baixiu.'

'Hold me.' She leaned up against me. 'Treat me the way you treated her.'

Her body, draped in the grey dress, pressed itself tightly up against my chest, trembling, as if she would slip out of my grip.

5

Ah, Miss Baixiu, I feel like crying.

We each carried our own, very different sad past, and yet we were still able to hold each other so intensely.

A normal man wouldn't be able to resist such impassioned feelings, and it would be impossible for him to remain clear-headed and guilt-free. But I was feeble, unlike a normal man, and I could only put my arms around you; I don't know if my senseless sobbing served as a response. All I can say is, my weakness had nothing to do with love; on the contrary, I was able to stop at the last minute precisely because I understand what love is all about.

Love of every kind has a critical point, and crossing that line will result in great losses.

Miss Baixiu, your father can serve as a good example for casually crossing that line. He'd been a decent, honest man, but one moment of loneliness and lustful feelings unfortunately led him across the chasm, and he realized that the road ahead would be tortuous. Qiuzi did the same thing, but, sadly, she did it for me. If she hadn't been so eager to raise money, she wouldn't have covered her eyes and taken that leap at the critical point, no matter how naïve she was or how many ruses your father used.

All I can say is, the ruse was too intricate, like a deep hole edged with lace, or an abyss filled with trust. I cannot even imagine how frightening it must have been for a normally timid girl in the instant she covered her eyes and jumped. It breaks my heart to think about the internal struggles she must have faced; it makes me feel similarly shackled.

Regrettably, at that helpless instant, I, too, reached a critical point and I, too, crossed the line without thinking – I had mistakenly believed that everything she had lost belonged to me. Therefore, though I wept, I didn't try to stop her on that morning when she walked out, and, as a consequence, I lost even more.

I've lost everything that I could see, including a credit loan, which you probably didn't know. When the kidnappers got away with the money, I didn't own a single thing the bank could seize in recompense. I had got money in one hand and it went out from the other, like a joke in this comical life, or like the shattering of my childhood dreams.

And yet, in the midst of this laughable situation you shocked me, Miss Baixiu; your arms were so warm they gave me such happy sorrow I nearly lost control. 'Can I do this?' I was thinking at the time, and instead of dodging, I slyly tightened my arms around you, and the embrace was suddenly laden with euphoric fantasy. I didn't want to let go. The existence of this kind of love was a bit of a shock to me, for you were able to break through your father's anguish and press up close to me. I wished I'd enjoyed embraces like that from my childhood on – then perhaps I could have led a happy life despite Qiuzi's absence.

But it came too late.

I will continue to wait for her in whatever corner I may wind up, simply because I have yet to reveal to her the ending of a story, a story about a goat. I'd wanted to give that goat to my father, towards whom I'd harboured resentment, but it was stolen. A very simple ending. My life story could very well be condensed into the tale of a goat. A man's sorrow really should not be so inconsequential, yet it can never disappear once it seizes his life, precisely because it is so insignificant.

Qiuzi is the goat in my life, Miss Baixiu.

Now I know she will never come. At this moment I am walking along the levee in early winter; the reeds wear white tips all the way to the beach. I didn't come here for the ocean view, however. I will get off the levee at the hairpin bend, where the waves crash loudly, then follow the path across the bridge, all the way down to the Catholic church in the town centre. There is a park nearby, the starting point for your father on his bicycle that day. Your house is just around the corner, behind the park.

I've come for one last look at the cherry tree, Miss Baixiu.

I have done so despite the fact that you no longer have a cherry tree and I have lost Qiuzi for ever.

So I will be standing outside your house in a few minutes, but I won't knock at the door. I just want one more look at it to find a burial site for my lowly suffering. Yet I am a little nervous; I didn't know that breaking free from one of life's predicaments could be so hard – if I ran into your father at that moment, should I take cover to avoid frightening him or should I stay put and let myself tremble pitifully?

By now I am down from the levee, and the waves around the bend are deafening. Your father turned in from the bridge that day, and must have been listening to the surf along the way. He smiled so gracefully as he stopped outside the coffee shop. Of course he would be smiling. But can any tide be so pleasing to the ears when it is nothing but waves that cannot find a beach?

I terminated the lease earlier at noon, Miss Baixiu, and gave everything to the landlord. I will get on a bus and leave town this evening, vanishing like the cherry tree that disappeared from your house.

I detest the ocean.